The Holiday Season

MICHAEL
KNIGHT

The Holiday Season

Grove Press
New York

Published simultaneously in Canada
Printed in the United States of America

FIRST EDITION

ISBN-10: 0-8021-1857-7
ISBN-13: 978-0-8021-1857-8

Grove Press
an imprint of Grove/Atlantic, Inc.
841 Broadway
New York, NY 10003

Distributed by Publishers Group West

www.groveatlantic.com

07 08 09 10 11 12   10 9 8 7 6 5 4 3 2 1

For George Garrett

Contents

The Holiday Season

A sad tale's best for winter.
—William Shakespeare,
The Winter's Tale

Part 1: Thanksgiving

That first full winter of the new millennium, the holiday season in particular, was an awkward time in the history of us Poseys. My mother was three years dead and my father was still bewildered by the loose ends of his retirement, and my brother, Ted, who had a wife and twin daughters and a brand-new house in Point Clear, had decided that this was the year his family needed to start establishing some traditions of their own. Ted tried to include us, of course, extended several invitations, but in the end, Dad couldn't be persuaded to leave Mobile for Thanksgiving. I suggested that Ted bring the girls over for a visit the day before or the day after, whatever he wanted, but he felt provoked by our father's obstinance and he, too, refused to bend. Telling it now, the whole business reeks of pettiness and folly, but like most family squabbles, it seemed important at the time.

I could just as easily begin this account in a more overtly momentous year: 1994—the year of my father's failed campaign for the U.S. House of Representatives. 1996—the year the twins were born. 1997—my mother's last year on earth. But in a way that's difficult to articulate, those final months of that first year of the brand-new millennium marked a culmination of all those things. In memory, the intervening years seem a sort of holding pattern, after the dust had settled on significant events, but before life cranked back up again in earnest. Though there was hardly an hour door to door between Ted's new house and our old place on Mohawk Street, I couldn't help imagining my father and my brother faced off across Mobile Bay like distant nations on the brink of war.

So it was under these circumstances that I found myself pitching horseshoes with my father on the last Wednesday in November. It was early evening, unseasonably warm even for lower Alabama, light melting down through the branches of the trees. I watched Dad draw back, slowly, slowly, watched him let a horseshoe fly, watched the horseshoe catch an edge and cartwheel past the stake.

In a discouraged voice, he said, "What are we playing to again?"

The ground was littered with fallen leaves, brown and brittle, all curled in upon themselves. I thought maybe I should rake tomorrow, wondered if he'd raked at all this year.

"Eleven," I said.

"I used to be good at this." He rubbed his eyes, gazed over the chain link fence. There was a little yellow house back there, an old woman puttering on her back porch. "We'll visit your mother in the morning," Dad said, meaning her grave.

We walked the length of the pit, toeing the ground in search of wayward horseshoes. The leaves were that deep. Down in the mulchy yellow grass, I spotted the ID tag from a pet collar. The lettering had weathered off. I showed him what I'd found but he just shrugged.

"It's five o'clock," he said. "I need a drink."

And he trudged off toward the house without another word. I sat on the ground to wait for him, rubbed the ID tag between my fingers. You could hardly feel the traces of engraving there. Hardy the Lab, Mullet the mutt, Salmon P. Chase the cat. The long-gone pets of my youth. It was hard to believe the tag could have belonged to any of them, could have remained undiscovered in the backyard all that time. My father drove those horseshoe stakes when I was nine years old. That was nearly a quarter century ago.

Behind me, I heard a woman calling, "Allo-o." There was plenty of French accent in her voice. "Ooo is that I see?"

I stood and faced the voice and saw the old woman closing fast from her side of the fence.

"You must be the son," she said. "Ted, no?"

I told her, "I'm the other one," and I would have sworn she looked disappointed. She was my father's age, maybe a little younger. It was hard to tell. She wore her hair in a silver-blond pageboy and her features were all pinched together in the middle of her face.

"Frank," I said.

The woman extended her hand. Her fingers were limp and knotty in mine.

"Madame Langlois. I am you father's neighbor." She pointed behind her at the little yellow house. "You look like your father very much."

"He's inside," I said.

Madame Langlois fingered the collar of her turtleneck, a gesture made girlish by the tilt of her head and by the fact that her nails were painted prom-dress pink. "Your father, he is a good man." Her accent was like something from the movies, all bouncy pitch and rounded vowels, her S's edged with Z's. "There are not so many like him willing to dedicate themselves to—how you say?—public service." She bobbed her head to underscore the words.

What she said was true. My father was a twelve-term city councilman, an important man in his way, dedicated, locally connected. There were photographs of him with Jimmy Carter, with Mike Dukakis, with Bill Clinton hanging in the room we had always called his "den." The Clinton photo was taken in 1994, the year Dad ran for Congress. The president was in town stumping for local Democrats. Likely his endorsement hurt more than it helped in this part of the world.

Mohawk Street was located in an older part of the city known simply and practically as Midtown—halfway between the bars and the business district and the ship-yards down near where the river met the bay and on the other side, the more upscale neighborhoods in west Mobile, the country club, the private schools and so on. My father moved us there when I was six years old in an effort to expose his sons to more diversity. To an old Southern liberal like my father, diversity meant black people, and he wanted to see his boys riding bikes and playing ball with a more colorful group than was handy in west Mobile. Much to his dismay, however, lots of well-intentioned white folk had the same idea and the neighborhood began to gentrify around us al-most as soon as we moved in, new paint glistening on the shotgun houses and Creole cottages, contractors banging away all day long, landscapers' trucks parked along the curb. The net effect was to drive property values up and most of the black residents to the other, less pallid side of Government Boulevard. The house had tripled in value since Dad bought it and Ted was always pushing him to sell, maybe buy a condo on the bay, closer to him and Marcy and the girls, and sock the rest into a mutual fund or something, set him up big time in his retirement, but Dad refused. He claimed both inertia and nostalgia but I think he was embarrassed by how much the house was worth. I think he was waiting around for the neighborhood to go to pot again.

In an effort, perhaps, to expedite the process, he'd let the old place fall into disrepair, both inside and out. The toilets ran. The paint was chipped. The gutters sagged. The floors needed refinishing. The shutters were missing slats. This was not to mention nonstructural wreckage, the pile of *New Yorkers* in the foyer, the discarded undershirts and boxer shorts on the bathroom floor, the unwashed dishes in the sink, all of which seemed somehow to emanate, like fallout, from the den.

That's where I tracked him down after parting ways with Madame Langlois. He was pretending to sleep in his recliner but I could tell he was awake. His face was alert even though his eyes were closed. A single lamp was burning beside the chair, spotlighting him, accentuating shadows, making the scene look staged. He had the TV tuned to the news, the volume muted.

"Dad?"

I flicked on the overhead.

He stretched and faked a yawn. "Did you say something? I just turned this on to see the weather. I guess I dozed off. That's what happens when you get old."

I tossed yesterday's *Press Register* on the floor to make room on the couch. The other cushions were strewn with men's dress socks, maybe three dozen, brown, black, blue, argyle, none of them balled into a pair. The room was a sort of quintessential den, with its wood paneling, its furniture banished from other, better rooms. Mom always kept her distance, partly, I suppose, to allow Dad a sanctuary in the house but also because the room had reached, long before she died, an irreversible momentum toward decay.

"Your neighbor dropped by."

I watched his face, his eyes.

"Which one?"

He brought the recliner upright with a hand lever, patted his pockets for his glasses, got them situated. There was a tumbler of scotch sweating on the end table. I was pretty sure the timing of his exit was deliberate. He knew exactly who I meant.

"The French one," I said.

"Is she gone? What did she want?"

I sniffed a blue sock to see if it was clean. "I don't know. Just to talk to you, I guess. To introduce herself to me." I pushed my hand up in the sock and worked it like a puppet. "Sounds like you guys are pretty friendly."

My father made a face.

"That woman's nuts," he said.

~

We ordered pizza for dinner and when there was nothing left but rinds of crust, I suggested a game of chess. We Poseys have always played games—horseshoes, chess, backgammon, poker, darts, croquet—to pass the time. We set up on the breakfast table. By the time the doorbell rang, maybe half an hour later, my father had slugged two more scotches and played me into a corner. It was just after nine o'clock. I padded through the darkened dining room, dodging furniture by memory, catching my knee on an umbrella stand. There was Madame Langlois on the stoop, bearing a Tupperware container.

"I brought you a cake," she said. "It is nothing. I was baking."

Without waiting for an invitation, Madame Langlois retraced my route through the dining room to the kitchen, but my father was gone when we arrived. She surveyed the room, took in the chess pieces still poised, the pizza box on the counter. I could hear the shower running upstairs, the rattle and groan of old plumbing. Madame Langlois turned on her heel.

"It is poppy seed and lemon," she said.

I thanked her, told her that she shouldn't have, but Madame Langlois waved my gratitude away. She opened the refrigerator, scanned the shelves. There was hardly anything in there (I'd already decided to go shopping in the morning) but Madame Langlois hesitated with her cake as if searching for space. She made a pensive, puckery sound, then faced me again, the cake at her shoulder like a waitress.

"Listen to me," she said. "I can see that you are helpless. You must let me cook for you tomorrow night."

"I thought I'd take Dad out."

"*Non,*" said Madame Langlois. "The holiday, it is about the home. The turkey and the pilgrims and the giving thanks."

I almost laughed. "That's too much trouble."

"I insist," she said. "It is final. No more talking. My family is, how you say . . . ?" She fluttered her hand. I had no idea what expression she was looking for so she finished the thought herself. "I am alone. I have no plans."

That's where the trouble always started with me. I liked this woman—her overcooked accent, her aggressive loneliness—and I wanted, just then, to make her happy. Plus, I'm sure part of me was worried about being alone with Dad, worried we'd both be miserable. The whole thing was purely selfish. Though I could sense repercussions looming, I shunted all thoughts of the future aside and accepted her invitation. I walked her out, feeling pleased with myself, then headed upstairs to check in with Dad.

"I'm in the shower," he shouted. "What do you want?"

I tried the knob, unlocked. I poked my head in so we could hear each other better. He was perched on the toilet, fully dressed. A look of panic washed over his face, then anger, then resignation. Finally, his features settled into sheepish. I'd never seen him look sheepish in his life.

"What's going on, Dad?"

"Nothing," he said. "Nothing's going on."

I told him about Madame Langlois's visit, about the plans we'd made, and my father pushed abruptly to his feet. "No. No. I will not have my Thanksgiving with that woman."

He dropped his shoulder, brushed past me out the door. I followed him to his room down the hall. To my surprise, the room was immaculate, a perfect contrast to the rest of the house: the bed neatly made, no clothes scattered on the floor. Even his loose change was stacked in little piles atop the dresser—pennies, nickels, dimes, quarters. My mother was always on him about picking up after himself.

"C'mon, Dad," I said. "She's nice. She's all alone."

"She's a nuisance," my father said.

On what used to be my mother's nightstand, I noticed a long, red wig, the color of stained cedar, on one of those Styrofoam heads. She'd bought lots of wigs during her run of chemo but I was pretty sure that this one was the last. It was creepy, seeing it there like that, made my joints all watery.

I told him, "It's too late to cancel," but there was no resolve left in my voice.

"It's not. Go over there right this minute. It's not too late. Tell her anything you want."

"I can't."

"Please."

His eyes were round, bloodshot, his hair mussed like he'd been asleep. My father had gone gray years ago and he had these wild white eyebrows. My mother used to say his eyebrows put her in mind of a demented genius but just then he resembled nothing so much as a tired, old man. I didn't see how I could refuse him.

Madame Langlois answered the door in a white silk bathrobe with what looked like peacock feathers on the lapel. She smiled, blinked, clutched her robe across her chest. Her chest was mottled with liver spots and right away I knew I couldn't go through with breaking the date. My father would be furious, but I'd figure something out. The question now was what to tell her about why I'd come.

"*Bonsoir,*" she said. "Come in, come in. You will excuse my appearance, *s'il vous plaît.* I wasn't expecting anyone."

I followed her to the living room and she waved me into a chair, offered me tea? brandy? a little wine? I said no thanks. Madame Langlois settled herself on a chaise longue. The room was spare but tasteful, everything antique, old books in the built-in shelves. The whole house smelled of cooking. Not just baking but the savory aroma of meat warming in the oven. Was it possible she'd already started preparing for tomorrow?

"Do you have pets?" I said.

"*Oui.*" She pointed at a birdcage draped with a pale blue sheet, drew her knees up. Her shins were practically translucent. "My parakeet, Abigail. She is asleep."

"It's just that I found an ID tag—you know, like for a dog collar. I thought maybe you might have lost it—your pet I mean."

"Abigail does not wear a collar."

"Right." I felt a blush coming on. "It would only apply if you had a dog or cat. Whatever. Maybe you know if one of the neighbors is missing something like that?"

"This is why you've come?"

I cleared my throat.

"Well."

Madame Langlois reached over to pat my knee.

"Tell me about yourself," she said. "I know about your brother. The lawyer." She accented the second syllable instead of the first making Ted's profession sound suddenly exotic. "The father of Jeff's grandchildren. Twins, yes? But I know only that you exist."

"He talks about Ted?"

"Your father is very proud."

I turned thirty-three years old that year. I was single and without prospects. When people asked me what I did for a living, I told them I was a member of Shakespeare Express, this theater group that traveled around to high schools all over the South, doing half-hour versions of *Hamlet* or *Romeo and Juliet* or a sort of greatest hits compilation, the big, dramatic moments from the most popular plays, anything we could cram into the time allotted for a school assembly. I hated it but how else was I supposed to pay the bills? I also performed at The Playhouse over on Spring Hill Avenue. That past summer I'd done Vince in *Buried Child*, which sounded, at least to me, more legitimate than Shakespeare Express but paid less well than delivering pizzas. Now and then I had a date or two with one of the actresses from whatever show I was working on. Sometimes we had sex. I mention this only because, given the specifics of my life, people often assumed that I was gay. The rest of the story is that I tried New York after college and failed and when I came home I thought I'd figure out some other way to make a living. I never did. Here's the point: I understood, despite the holiday dustup, why my father would be more likely to discuss Ted's life than mine, but still it took the wind out of me a little.

This time, when I got home, he really was dozing in his recliner, mouth hanging open, chin slick with drool, the TV blaring CNN. His face looked thin and pale. There was a half-empty scotch between his legs, his right hand capped over the glass, as if to keep foreign objects out while he was asleep. I worried that he was drinking too much and thought maybe I should talk to him about it but Dad had always liked a drink and it was a holiday besides—certainly not the time. So I woke him up and waited for him to get oriented. He wouldn't let me help him up to bed.

I'd planned to go on home and come back in the morning but I made up my mind then and there to spend the night. It seemed like the right thing. And

my place wasn't much besides. I was on the road
enough that it didn't make sense to spend a lot on rent
so I kept a room in what amounted to a boardinghouse
here in town. I liked the idea of sleeping in my old
bed. The posters and pennants on the walls, all left over
from my boyhood. The musty blankets. There was still
a working phone on the nightstand. I wasn't ready to
pack it in so I called Ted.

"It's late," he said, after I'd identified myself.
"We've got kids here, pal. The girls are out by eight
o'clock."

"I just wanted to check in."

"How's Dad?"

"He's all right," I told him. "A little down, you
know, but all right. Don't forget to call tomorrow."

In my pocket, I found the ID tag. I'd forgotten it
was there.

"I'm not an idiot," he said.

"It's just that you sounded pissed last week."

"To be honest, I was pissed. I am pissed. I think
I have a right to be pissed that my father doesn't want
to visit his granddaughters on Thanksgiving. We've
come to him every holiday since the girls were born. I
miss Mom, too, but I have a family to think about. It's
been three years." Ted paused, took a breath. "And
you're not doing anybody any good humoring him.
You should be here, Frank, not holding his hand. I'm

your brother. You haven't even been over to check out my new house."

"I've been busy. I've been out of town."

"Yeah," he said. "Right. He's a grown man, Frank. You're both grown men."

I stretched out on the bed, clipped the ID tag between my teeth. How familiar all this was—the spongy mattress, the window leaking a draft over my feet, my brother's voice on the phone, my father snoring down the hall. Ted and I had shared that room until he went away to the University of Alabama. I'd gotten in the habit back then of calling him after everyone else had gone to bed, listening to his adventures, fraternity stuff and stuff with girls, nothing major, but it all seemed foreign and magical at the time.

"I guess."

Ted said, "It's true."

"He's got this neighbor. This crazy French lady."

There passed a stretch of silence on the line.

"I fail to see the relevance," Ted said.

In the morning, as promised, we visited my mother's grave. It was cooler than the day before, cold enough to mist our breath, a suggestion that winter might at last be on its way to Alabama. Dad didn't say a word about me sleeping over. For a long time, we stood there without speaking. I tried to think about Mom, tried to pray but I didn't know what to ask of God. She was or was not in heaven by now and I had all these mixed feelings about religion to begin with. I tried, after a while, to empty my mind, to pay homage to my mother with silent meditation, but life kept creeping in. I couldn't quit thinking about Ted, wondering if he was sorry that he wasn't coming for Thanksgiving, and I was worried about what to tell Dad about Madame Langlois.

My mother was originally from Baton Rouge, a big, Cajun-looking woman, dark hair, dark eyes, broad shoulders, just over six feet tall, though she disliked her size and lied about it on her driver's license. She moved to Mobile to take a job at the Planned Parenthood Center here. The work was trying and turnover was quick and my mother was bright and capable. She was managing the center inside two years. That's how she met my father. He was still practicing law back then, had agreed to do some pro bono stuff for Planned Parenthood. Decades later, when the cancer forced her out of work, Mom said to me, "The good news is I've seen the last of all those stupid, careless girls." I'm still not sure if she was kidding. There was real bitterness in her voice. At the time, I believed she was angry at her illness, not her job, but I don't know. That kind of work, there's never any end in sight. It can't help but wear a person down. In old pictures, the first thing you notice is my mother's carriage, how proud-looking she was, how erect, even with two young sons hanging on her like chimpanzees. But her height worked against her over time and even before she got sick, she was stooping a little, as if leaning into wind.

Back on the road, headed home, I asked, apropos of nothing, why Dad didn't take another crack at national office. It's not like he lost in a landslide. His opponent nipped him by 4 percent.

"Well," he said, then he went quiet a moment, gathered his thoughts. He kept his eyes on the windshield. "You have to remember I'd already been on the city council a long time so I'd made plenty of enemies. Even in the party. Plus, this district is pretty conservative, you know that. They wanted a moderate to run against the Nazis that pass for Republicans in this part of the state. Plus, I'm sixty-six years old." He switched on the radio, spun the dial, turned it off. "Plus, your mother—she was pretty disappointed."

When they got married, Dad had just hung out a shingle and he was taking a lot of court-appointed cases to stay afloat. The way I understood it, it was Mom's idea for him to run for city council, not to win necessarily but to get his name out there, to give him a forum, which might drum up better-paying business. But he did win, to their surprise, and it turned out he liked having a say in how his city worked. I wondered if Congress wasn't her idea as well.

We drove a while in silence, past a church, a pawnshop, a Burger King. Then it was my father's turn for non sequitur.

"Your brother is a lucky man," he said.

"How's that?"

"He's making money hand over fist and he's got Marcy. I hope he knows how lucky he is."

I thought about my brother's wife, how beautiful she was, how unflappable with Ted and the girls. And I thought about the twins, Lily and Colleen, each a lovely and perfect replica of the other. And I thought about my brother, too, how he was always telling me, without actually saying the words aloud, that it was high time to get serious about my life.

I said, "You had Mom."

"Your mother, who lived her whole life right, died at sixty. That's not luck."

I could imagine several replies, all of them having to do with how fortunate my father was to have found someone to love at all, but it didn't make sense to argue. I considered broaching the subject of Madame Langlois but before I could speak, my father bolted forward in his seat.

"Turn here," he said. "Here. Quick."

I followed his directions through a four-way stop.

"Where are we going?"

"I want to show you something. I was visiting your mother not too long ago and got turned around on the way home so I'm not a hundred percent. It's here somewhere." He was sitting on the edge of his seat, hands on the dashboard, eyes scanning out the window. "There," he said. "Take this right." He directed me to a nondescript brick rancher, told me to pull over at the curb. He was out of the car and on the lawn before I had time to kill the engine. It took a moment to realize what it was he wanted me to see: what looked like a dollhouse in the grass, plantation style, maybe four feet tall, a miniature Cadillac parked out front.

When I opened my door, I heard Elvis doing "Spanish Harlem."

"It's Graceland," my father said.

"It's what?"

"Look in the windows. It's an exact replica. The jungle room. The bathroom where he died. It's Graceland down to the last detail."

I walked over and peeked inside. There was an Elvis doll in a sequined Vegas jumpsuit sprawled on a tiny leather couch, feet propped up like he was winding down after a show.

"You're kidding me," I said.

"It's up year-round. They pipe music in and everything." Dad pointed at a speaker on a corner of the rancher. "Twenty-four hours a day, though I understand they turn the volume down at night. The neighbors just got used to it, I guess. I talked to the owners last time I was here. The wife grew up in Memphis. Nice people. Love Elvis, of course. They voted for me many times."

"I have no idea what to think about this."

"Isn't it perfect?" my father said.

Elvis sounded deep and sad as ever, just about right for that late November morn.

While he napped, I raked and bagged and contemplated my father in his retirement. Dad made up his mind to call it quits in 1998, near the end of his last term, and his decision took everybody by surprise—his colleagues, his secretary, his sons most of all. He was still a young man, relatively speaking, and he had nothing particular in mind for the rest of his life and he refused to give anybody a reason. When we asked, he'd go on about how he was fully vested in his pension plan and we didn't have anything to worry about. At first he took some pro bono cases and advised other lawyers now and then in their dealings with the city and I was happy for him. It looked like he was getting back to where he started in the world. That was something I could understand. At some point, however, he quit working altogether (it took Ted and me a while to arrive at this conclusion) and what I couldn't figure was how he filled his days. He had no hobbies to speak of. Most of his friends were still employed so he wasn't hanging out with them. I didn't want to ask him what he did with all his time. It seemed intrusive, potentially embarrassing, but I was concerned. I had an image of him lounging in his recliner, drinking scotch in the middle of the day and watching the world go by on CNN.

When I finished the leaves, I headed for Winn-Dixie, loaded up on basics: soup and cereal, bread and fruit, coffee and milk. That's all Dad ever bothered with by himself, and pretty much all I could afford besides.

Afterward, I stopped off at my place to pick up a change of clothes. I lived in a converted Victorian on Dauphin Street, four bedrooms in all, two up, two down, with a communal kitchen and TV room. The landlady, Mrs. Mauldin, kept one of the downstairs bedrooms for herself, some kind of tax dodge, a way to write off the mortgage or something, but she had another residence in Maryland and was hardly ever around. Next to her lived a deaf woman named Chloe Jones. She was always talking to herself, narrating, I supposed, her interior life. "I don't know about hot dogs," she might say when I passed her in the hall, her deaf woman's voice all loud and glottal. Or, "I wish I was left-handed." I figured it had something to do with her inability to hear, with the way she negotiated between thought and word and sound, but it's possible she was merely strange.

My room was on the second floor, down the hall from Lucious Son. He didn't have a job as far as I could tell and he always had people coming and going and the air seeping out from under his door reeked so frequently of pot I was pretty sure that's how he paid his rent.

Lucious was practicing martial arts in the parking lot when I pulled in. His father was Korean, he'd told me, his mother from Trinidad, his fighting style a hybrid of techniques they'd taught him as a boy. He swiveled his hips and snaked his arms and hopped from foot to foot. None of it looked particularly dangerous.

"Gimme some of that good stuff," he said as I stepped out of the car.

I thought about it for a second. The leafless trees. The pewter sky. The weird kung fu.

I said, "We few, we happy few, we band of brothers / For he today that sheds his blood with me / Shall be my brother; be he ne'er so vile / This day shall gentle his condition / And gentlemen in England now a-bed

/ Shall think themselves accursed they were not here / And hold their manhood cheap whiles any speaks / Who fought with us upon Saint Crispin's day."

He'd overheard me rehearsing after I moved in and now he made requests.

"That's what I'm talking about," he said.

He balanced on one foot, palmed his fist at about the level of his belly button and gave me a bow.

I went on up to my room. There wasn't much to look at. The old pine desk, the bookshelves stuffed with paperbacks, the scuffed and rugless hardwood floor. The radiator was off and it was cold. It felt like nobody had been in there for a long time.

Dad started in on me as soon as I got home.

"What the hell?" he said. "What's wrong with you? I can't believe you lied." I mean his eyes were bulging, hands waving in the air. He caught me so off guard that it took a minute to get my head around what happened. Turned out Madame Langlois had called while I was gone to propose a change of plans: She was still cooking but she wanted to eat at our house instead of hers.

"Goddamnit, Frank." He followed me out to my Subaru while I retrieved another load of groceries. "You promised. I sounded like a fool."

I noticed then that he was holding a pair of penny loafers in his left hand, fingers hooked into the heels, like he'd meant to put them on but was so anxious to let me have it that he'd forgotten. His toenails were long and yellow. I thought his feet were probably cold. My car was ping-ping-pinging about its open door.

I said, "Look, I'm sorry. You should have seen her. All alone in this robe. It had feathers on it, Dad. I couldn't do it."

He just stared. Nothing can make you feel more like somebody's kid than that look of disappointment. Then he stomped back up to the house and I started lugging the groceries in myself, thinking I was supposed to be there to spend time with my father, not humor Madame Langlois, thinking no way did a thing like this happen on my brother's watch. That's when the bottom tore out of one of the bags and three cantaloupes went bowling down the driveway. I managed to catch up to the first one but the second veered off and disappeared into the gutter, while the third raced toward Mohawk, where it exploded beneath the tires of a passing SUV.

～

Four o'clock found me cleaning house. I'd always thought there was something sad about that hour, that season. It had to do with early nightfall and the encroachment of another year. Dad was holed up in his room with the door locked. I did the best I could but the vacuum cleaner didn't work and I couldn't find a dustpan and the house was pretty far gone besides. Mostly, I wound up hiding the mess in closets and under furniture or trying to organize it (what else was I supposed to do with all those back issues of the *New Yorker?*) into a neater semblance of itself. Madame Langlois was due at 5:30 and it was way too late to put her off and I had no ideas. I thought about calling Ted. He'd never have admitted it but I knew it would make him happy to hear that Thanksgiving had gone to hell without him, and I was pretty sure he'd know how to make things right, but I was embarrassed and I didn't want to give him the pleasure. He was probably sitting down right that minute to a beautifully set table with his beautiful wife and his beautiful little girls, all of them done up like something from a Brooks Brothers catalog. Or maybe they'd already finished the meal and the house had settled into nap time, a fire burning toward embers in the hearth, a football game on TV with the volume turned down low. It was cheesy, sure, but it was so bewitching in my imagination that I was jealous of Ted and irritated with Dad for his unwillingness to compromise.

Eventually, I gave up on the house and trudged upstairs, knocked on my father's door. No answer, but

I could hear NPR ticking off the headlines on his clock radio.

"Dad?"

Nothing.

"Do you think Ted voted for Bush?" I said.

I knew the answer and so did Dad but we'd just come through a messy election and I hoped politics would provoke a response. Ted's politics in particular. I pressed my ear to the door. Somehow, the faint droning of the radio made the silence more pronounced.

I said, "I know Marcy has a sticker on her Suburban," but Dad held out.

Back downstairs, I hunted up matching place mats, set the table for three just in case. I found some candles in the pantry. By the time I was finished, it was 5:15. Still no sign of Dad. I decided to tell Madame Langlois he wasn't feeling well. It'd be just the two of us tonight. To steel myself, I poured a great big scotch and sat at the table, took a minute to catch my breath. I was wondering if there was more to my father's reasons for avoiding Madame Langlois than personal distaste—he seemed almost afraid of her— when Dad himself appeared in the doorway, wearing a blazer and tie. His hair was wet-combed like a kid.

"I need one of those," he said, aiming a finger at my drink.

~

Madame Langlois was right on time. It took the three of us two trips to haul all that food in from her car. Turkey on a silver platter. Sweet potatoes. Stuffing. Bread. Some kind of fish and mushroom casserole in a Pyrex dish. Salad in a huge plastic bowl. She had made both pumpkin and pecan pie. She insisted that Dad and I take our places at the table while she did the final preparations.

From the kitchen, Madame Langlois said, "I hope you do not mind. The casserole, it is French. I know this is your holiday but I love to see my American friends enjoy French food."

She said *eet* instead of *it*. Her accent seemed some-how even thicker than before.

I waited a second, gave my father a chance to reply. He didn't bother. Before I could speak, Madame Langlois was running on again.

"I had the most wonderful day in the kitchen. It gives me such a pleasure to cook for men with their appetites."

Zee, she said. *Geeves*.

I cut a look at my father, tried, with an eyebrow thing and a complicated smile, to let him know that I was in on the joke—sure, she was ridiculous—but also gratified that he and I had been able to make her happy in this small way. He looked away, sipped at the sauvignon blanc she'd poured. He screwed his face up at the taste and went back to scotch instead.

"Your mother," he said, "she used to drink merlot with everything. Red meat, white meat. It didn't matter. She knew what she liked. She'd put a single ice cube in. She preferred it just a little chilled and watered down."

An egg timer dinged and I heard a tiny continental-sounding exclamation from Madame Langlois.

Dad went on. "She never liked a turkey at Thanksgiving. You remember? Too cliché. We'd do beef tender instead. She wasn't much of a cook but it always turned out nice."

He was talking like Mom had been gone for decades, like he was worried I'd forgotten her. His voice was way too loud.

There was some banging and rustling in the kitchen. A minute later Madame Langlois swung into the room bearing the turkey platter, which she placed on a trivet beside my father. She lifted the lid with a flourish. It was a beautiful bird.

"You will carve for us, Jeff, no?"

My father grunted his assent and Madame Langlois shuttled in a few more platters, then took her seat across from me. She looked a little wilted. We watched Dad hack at the turkey.

"So," she said. "Tell me, Frank. You have been to France?"

I bobbed my head. "After college. I did the back-pack thing."

"How long were you in my country?"

"Let's see—Paris for about a week," I said, "then the south, Nice and Antibes. Maybe two weeks altogether."

Madame Langlois served herself some casserole, started the dish on its round. "You did not visit the Loire Valley?"

"Afraid not."

I took some, passed the casserole to my father and waited for Madame Langlois to finish with the salad. She made a little sucking sound with her tongue. "Then you did not see France. The Loire Valley is the very—how you say?—the very soul of the country. My father and his father before him and on and on like so, they had a vineyard near Lyon."

Right then, my father slapped the serving spoon into the casserole dish, hard enough to splatter his tie and the lenses of his glasses.

"That's it," he said. "I can't listen to this." He glared at us, didn't seem to notice the dollop of cream sauce obscuring his left eye. "This woman," he said, bolting to his feet and aiming a finger like a TV law-yer. "She's from North goddamn Carolina. Her father may have run a vineyard but what he made was third-rate domestic cabernet." Madame Langlois's lips were pressed into a thin white line. My father addressed her directly. "You've been in this country almost fifty years." His voice leapt up in volume at the end of the sentence. "It's absurd. You're more American than Frank."

I wasn't sure what he meant by that. He turned, too quickly, tipping his chair back on its hind legs, and stormed off from the table. The chair wobbled a moment, righted itself. Because it was too awkward and confusing to meet each other's eyes, Madame Langlois and I stared at the space my father vacated like he'd vanished in a puff of smoke.

While I helped Madame Langlois pack all that food into Dad's refrigerator—she insisted, said she'd made it for us, said it was too much for her—she told me two stories.

The first confirmed a fair amount of my father's accusation while casting the details in a different light. It turned out that the Langlois family vineyard went belly-up when she was in her teens and her father was forced to take a job overseeing production at a fledgling winery in the States, the pet project of a poet who'd married an heiress and had the advantage of her money.

Her father wouldn't let his children (Madame Langlois was the youngest of three) speak English in the house, which explained, she said, the fact that she still had an accent after all this time. She'd come to Mobile to take a job teaching languages at the Jesuit college here in town.

I was beginning to wonder how my father had arrived at his knowledge of her past, when she launched, unbidden, into the second story. After months of cajoling, he'd accepted an invitation to dinner at her house. This was just before Halloween. Madame Langlois spared me no detail. The wine, the music, the candlelight. The food: smoked salmon soufflé, followed by fruit terrine. They talked, she about her father, he, after a while, about my brother. Madame Langlois was just setting a cup of coffee at his place when he took her face in both his hands and kissed her on the mouth.

"It was a perfect little kiss," she said.

Except that it caused her to forget herself so completely that she spilled the coffee in my father's lap. Except that once he recovered from the coffee he was embarrassed by the kiss and neither of them knew how to find their way back to intimacy. Dad had been vague and distant with her since.

When the food was put away, I walked her to her car and she rolled the window down.

"This is my fault," I said. "I'm sorry."

"But how could you have known?"

I couldn't help listening for traces of North Carolina in her voice. I put on an apologetic face.

"I ruined your Thanksgiving."

She shrugged.

"It is not my holiday," she said.

~

Inside, the phone was ringing and I snatched it up in the kitchen half a beat after my father answered upstairs.

I heard him say, "Jeff Posey," like he was at the office.

"Hey, Dad."

"Son," my father said, his voice thick with pleasure. Son, like Ted was an only child.

I was just about to hang up when Ted said, "Y'all eat yet?"

I hesitated. I wanted to know how Dad would answer, but he dodged the question like a pro.

"I bet Marcy really laid it on."

"I'm still stuffed," Ted said.

I knew I shouldn't be eavesdropping but I worried that if I hung up, they'd hear it, they'd find me out. Plus, I was curious. In the weeks leading up to Thanksgiving, I'd been acting as a go-between, getting accounts from each of them about what the other said. I hadn't seen or heard them together. To listen now, you would have thought nothing was wrong. My ear felt hot under the phone. I was interested, that's true. The two of them were maybe the most interesting things in my life.

Dad said, "The girls OK?"

"You bet," Ted said. "You'll see."

"Maybe you'll come at Christmas."

Ted was quiet.

Then he said, "Marcy's calling, Dad. I gotta run."

∼

People always described my mother as a "no- nonsense" woman and it was true. She never babied me or Ted or treated her clients at Planned Parenthood with kid gloves. She never hid the truth to spare somebody's feelings. She disliked public displays of affection. She disdained extravagance in almost any form. It wasn't that she was cold. I always knew she loved me and so, I'm sure, did Ted, and the girls down at the center seemed to appreciate that she wasn't full of shit. During Dad's run for the House, Mom told a reporter for the *Press Register* that she was almost certain her husband would lose. The piece was supposed to be a profile of the candidates' wives, something for the *Living* section, interior design photos and tender memories about the candidates. When the reporter asked why

Mom didn't like Dad's chances, she said, "Look, my husband has actually been doing his job all these years instead of cultivating influence with the business big shots and religious phonies, and it's been my experience that people like him hardly ever win elections anymore." Dad loved it, worked it into his campaign, though Ted told me later that he'd called in a favor with the editor (he was not altogether without influence, no matter what Mom said) to have the paper strike the next line of her quote, which read something like, "This is not to mention that most people around here think of me as a kind of back alley abortionist."

What I'm saying is I'm sure she would have wanted her husband to find comfort wherever he could when she was gone, even with someone as frivolous as Madame Langlois, but Dad didn't see it like that.

I was in the kitchen making a turkey sandwich when he finally came downstairs. He sat at the breakfast table and without asking, I prepared the sandwich the way he liked—salt and pepper, a little mayo; nothing fancy—and fixed him a scotch. I knew I shouldn't have but I did. He tucked in without a word and I set about making a second sandwich for myself.

"Everything all right?"

"Your brother called," he said.

"Yeah?"

He nodded, chewed.

"Tell me something," he said after a while. "Be honest now. What did you think about that miniature Graceland? You thought it was silly." He did a bashful grin. "Tell the truth."

"OK, sure. It was silly. Sure."

He shook his head. I carried my sandwich to the table, took my seat. Both of us had gotten more comfortable. I was in yesterday's jeans and a fleece pullover and Dad had put a robe on over his trousers and his undershirt.

"I don't want to stop loving your mother," he said.

That made me flinch. Dad took a bite, dropped his eyes. I tried to imagine what sort of feeling must have swept him up when he reached for Madame Langlois's face, touched his lips to hers, how his heart must have raced, how all the loneliness in the world must have been welling up inside him. I didn't know how much he might have overheard between me and Madame Langlois and I had no idea how to respond, but he wasn't after my opinion anyway.

"I'll fix it with Louise," he said.

"Who?"

"Madame Langlois."

"Oh," I said.

Somewhere, not too far off, a dog was barking. We listened for a second, then it stopped and a silence settled over us, neither awkward nor profound.

My father was the first to speak.

"Don't tell you brother about all this."

"Right," I said. "No problem."

When we finished eating, Dad freshened his drink and we adjourned to the den and watched three hours of a *Star Trek* marathon on TV. Halfway through the second episode, about a shape-shifting alien trying to commandeer the *Enterprise* by impersonating Captain Kirk, I looked over and saw that he'd been crying. Halfway through the third, I heard him snoring. Something was jabbing me in the leg and I rooted around in the pocket of my jeans and there was that pet ID tag from yesterday. It gave me an idea. I waited until the commercial, then crept out the front door and around the block to Madame Langlois's, slipped the tag into her mailbox. By way of apology. She'd know who left it there.

Elsewhere, my brother was in bed beside his lovely wife, his girls dreaming sweet dreams down the hall. Elsewhere, my mother knew all the secrets of the universe or nothing. Elsewhere, even at that late hour, Elvis was crooning to a tiny simulacrum of his life.

I found Dad right where I left him, an afghan in his lap, his glasses reflecting blue light from the TV.

This time, he let me help him up to bed.

Part 2: Christmas

Regarding holidays . . .

When I was a kid, I lived for Halloween and even very young I was heavily involved and invested in my costumes, but from ages six to eight, prime trick-or-treating years, I was stricken with a succession of illnesses serious enough that my parents forbade me from going out. First, strep throat, then mono, then an infection that caused both of my eyes to swell shut and baffled my pediatrician. It sprang up just forty-eight hours before the big night and was so mystifying (all Dr. Baldacci knew to do was prescribe antibiotics and send me to the hospital for tests, which turned up nothing) that I began to wonder if I hadn't done something to offend the cosmos. We never really went to church and my ideas about religion were a bit amorphous, but I'd picked up the basics. I lay in my bed, blind and scared, praying, if not for wellness then at least for an explanation. Why, God? Why me? Surely there was some other little boy who didn't care so much about Halloween.

The infection cleared up after a day or two without event or repercussions and what I remember best about that time is that for each of those three Halloweens my brother carried a Polaroid camera on his trick-or-treating route to record particularly interesting costumes and a pad and pen to keep track of who was giving out what sort of treats. He'd come into our room when he got home and sit on the bed and split his candy with me and tell me everything. It's possible that my parents put him up to it, though I have no evidence to prove it, and looking back, I'm sure a part of him took pleasure in rubbing my nose in what I'd missed, though if either of those things are true, he certainly never gave himself away. At the time, I thought he was very brave to sit with me like that, risking his health, and very generous to share his loot.

I mention this only because almost anything can seem meaningful in retrospect, deepened by the soft light and long shadows of the past, but that doesn't necessarily mean our lives are affected in the bare-bulb glare of the present. It seems to me sometimes that life is little more than a long string of missed opportunities and connections and we never know what a thing means until it's too late. Or that the meaning we attach is false, colored by faulty memory and wishful thinking. Or that we attach meaning to empty moments and miss the big picture altogether. What I'm trying to work up to here is that nothing much changed in the weeks between Thanksgiving and Christmas.

Dad went on moping around and Ted went on taking the hard line and I went on with my life more or
less exactly as before. I don't know if it would have
made a difference, but Ted and I didn't even talk about
Thanksgiving, not the details anyway, mostly, I think,
because Dad had sworn me to secrecy about Madame
Langlois, which made the rest of our time together
feel confidential as well. Because of the school holidays, Shakespeare Express was on hiatus, so I put in a
week at The Playhouse as Scrooge's nephew, Fred. I
shopped for presents. I went to parties. I slept alone.
And I decided, without much fanfare, to spend Christmas with my brother. I still hadn't made it over to
see his house and I'd given him plenty of excuses but
none of them held water with Ted, even if they were
genuine. I told myself that he was right, as usual, about
everything, that I really was doing more harm than
good with Dad, but the truth is Thanksgiving had
worn me out and it was tempting to imagine waking
up on Christmas morning in a house brimming with
good cheer.

I arrived just before dark on Christmas Eve and everybody came out to meet me in the yard. Marcy put the
twins through their paces: *Remember Uncle Frank? Give
your uncle Frank a hug.* They were blue-eyed like their

49

mother and fair-haired like their mother but somehow they looked like Ted. As if the weather had been special ordered by my brother, five inches of snow had sifted down the week before (still a record for that part of Alabama at that time of the year), then the temperature dropped below freezing and stayed there (also a record), so the world was icicle-y and white. We talked about that, how real winter always caught Alabama unprepared, then Ted and Marcy gave me the tour.

The house itself was modern looking, lots of picture windows, multiple rooflines, porches up and down, in the neighborhood of 5,000 square feet. Like a lot of places on Mobile Bay, it had a grand hallway running down the middle so you could see straight through from the front door to the silvery water out the back. When I was a kid, Point Clear was still quaint cottages and ramshackle bungalows along the boardwalk, summer places, but in the last twenty years it had become a kind of posh suburb of Mobile. Ted's neighbors were neurosurgeons and VPs and real estate investment guys, commuters all. Somewhere nearby lived a writer of modest fame. I knew Ted made plenty of money but he was only four years my senior and I was dazzled by the fact that he could pay for such a place.

My brother had started out doing defense work for a firm called Monk, Lewis and Fewer. He'd made his reputation on the strength of his performance in a lawsuit involving a train wreck in Bayou La Batre. Ted's firm represented the insurance company responsible for Black Belt Rail's liability policy. Fourteen people were killed, not so many for an accident like that, though more than enough to elicit a substantial punitive award, and the train was carrying a stew of toxic chemicals so that the bayou itself was thoroughly poisoned (scientists have pointed to that crash as the beginning of a significant decline in the local firefly population), and it looked to everyone but Ted like the best possible option was a quick settlement with minimal publicity. Because he is a good and thorough lawyer, however, because he doesn't put much stock in vagaries of popular opinion, Ted researched until he found a loophole in Black Belt's policy, something to do with maintenance and safety features. The loophole was tiny and well-concealed but big and real enough for the insurance company to sneak through without a scratch. They defaulted on the policy and the ensuing verdict bankrupted Black Belt Rail, putting over seven hundred jobs at risk and tying up in a Chapter 11 mess any damages Black Belt might have been able to pay, thus preventing nine widows, two widowers and three sets of grieving parents from collecting a dime. The insurance company was so impressed, in fact, that they dismissed Ted's firm and offered him a position as chief in-house counsel for the American Southeast. He bought the house around the first of November, three months after starting his new job, and here I was at last.

We were in the guest room now, Ted leaning in the doorway with my duffel in his hand, Marcy fluffing the pillows on what would be my bed. A row of windows looked out on the bay and I could see the wharf, Ted's boat out there on the lift, sleek and white, broad of beam, dangling six feet above the water like a trick of levitation.

"You're a lucky man," I said.

Ted said, "Welcome, little brother," and he slipped his free arm around Marcy's waist. They held the pose a moment, as if waiting for me to take their picture, before moving apart.

For dinner Marcy served shrimp bisque, followed by honeyed ham with English peas, and afterward she took the girls upstairs to get ready for bed while Ted and I retired to the living room with glasses of spiked eggnog. The ceilings were high enough that I half-expected our voices to come echoing back to us and there was a fire in the fireplace and a Christmas tree in the corner, all decked out and glittering, an abundance of pretty packages underneath. Though it was plenty warm inside, you could sort of sense the cold pressing in against the windows, making everything feel cozy and battened down. Ted was going on about our plans for the morning, presents and church and dinner and so on, but I mostly tuned him out. I closed my eyes and tipped my head back. I was sitting in a wingback chair, close enough to the fire that the heat was making me drowsy. I was trying not to think about Dad at the moment or about a decision I'd made that morning or about the fact that before too long I'd have to fill my brother in—trying, in short, and if only for a little while, to relax. Then I realized that my brother had stopped talking, and I peeked my left eye open. He was looking at me like he expected a reply.

"What's that?" I said.

Ted smirked and shook his head like inattention was to be expected of his little brother. Without answering, he took my glass and carried both of our drinks into the kitchen for a refill. He stood at the pass-through where I could see him, pouring from a clear glass pitcher, eggnog thick as paint.

"You talk to Dad?" he said.

I felt my shoulders tense. "Yesterday. I went over there." I took a breath. Now was as good a time as any to break the news. "I was thinking I might look in on him tomorrow. You know, after we eat."

Ted stopped pouring. "Would you come back?"

"He doesn't have a Christmas tree," I said.

53

I'd dropped by to do a surreptitious inventory of the fridge, make sure Dad wasn't roaring drunk or obviously depressed and found the corner by the bay window nothing more than its old self, all the lights and ornaments of my childhood still boxed up in the attic, and the sight had laid me low. I tried to talk Dad into letting me run up to a tree lot but he refused and for several hours, I'd seriously considered nixing Christmas altogether.

Ted pulled a sour face. "In the first place, Dad doesn't need a tree, and in the second, you can't stay just one night. We thought you'd at least be here til Monday. Marcy baked and everything. She made those cookies you like, those Mallomars or whatever."

My confusion must have been apparent because Ted paced over to the stairs, still holding the pitcher.

He shouted, "Marrrrcy?"

"What?" she shouted back.

"What do you call those cookies Frank likes? The ones I told you about. I'm drawing a blank."

"Macaroons," she said.

Ted turned back to me.

"I like macaroons," I said.

"Then it's settled." Marcy appeared suddenly on the landing, wrists draped over the banister, hair brushing her cheeks. "You'll stay until we're out of macaroons."

The twins were with her, ready for bed. They were wearing matching nightgowns. I could never tell which was which. Marcy whispered something in their ears and they hustled down the stairs and across the room and kissed me shyly and simultaneously on both cheeks, then retreated behind their father's legs. Ted said, "Tell your uncle Frank what you want for Christmas."

"A pony," they said in unison.

My brother laughed. "I keep telling them a pony will knock over furniture and leave road apples on the rug."

"It won't live in the house."

They were excited and exasperated at the same time and I had the idea that Ted had jumped them through these hoops before. I asked where it would live and without missing a beat, the twins said, "In the yard."

Marcy clapped her hands. "All right, girls. Santa won't do his thing unless you're both asleep."

"In separate beds," Ted said. "I'm gonna come check in a little while and I want everybody in her own bed."

I'd seen him with his kids, of course, but it still surprised me sometimes how completely Ted had given himself over to fatherhood. Maybe it was the house, so adult, so finished, if that's the word, the kind of place a man might live forever.

~

Turned out the twins were getting exactly what they wanted for Christmas. The ponies (there were two) were boarding on a farm out in the country. Ted had fixed it for somebody to bring them around in the morning before the girls woke up. He explained all this while Marcy was arranging Santa's payload around the tree, matching helmets and jodhpurs and riding boots, a pair of pony-sized English saddles.

"Technically," Ted said, "these are miniature horses. You know how Shetland ponies look like midgets? These guys have the right proportions."

In a pensive voice, Marcy said, "They're giving me the strangest dreams," and right away a look came over her face like what she'd said surprised her or like she hadn't meant to speak aloud.

My brother rolled his eyes.

"I'm in the mood for macaroons," he said, already headed for the kitchen. "Anybody else want macaroons?"

"No thank you," Marcy said.

They'd met in Ted's last year of law school. She was still an undergrad, a sophomore, as I recall, still Marcy Hammond then, Huntsville born and raised, daughter of a travel agent and a high school football coach. She majored in art history, minored in psychology and married my brother twenty-seven days after accepting her diploma.

"What about these dreams?" I asked.

She gave me a wary squint. "Do you really want to know?"

"I never remember dreams," I said.

I should probably admit that I used to call her now and then while my brother was at work. This was back when they were still living in Mobile. They were trying to get pregnant and Ted didn't see the point of Marcy's finding a job if she was just going to quit and I knew she was tired of shopping and lunches and movie magazines. Rehearsals were at night so my days were mostly empty, too. I'd bring her up to speed on all the theater gossip, if I was sleeping with one of the actresses or who was hooked on diet pills. Sometimes, when I wasn't on the road, I'd rent a movie and take it over there. The whole thing felt heady and illicit, like I was mixed up in an affair. Nothing ever happened, of course, and Ted knew all about it and I don't think I would have acted on my desire even if she'd been interested but in those days, the sight of her bare feet propped on the coffee table was enough to get me going. Naturally, I was happy for them when she got pregnant, but I was disappointed at the same time. Somehow, her pregnancy made our friendship untoward.

"Well," she said, "last night I dreamed I was a trick rider in the rodeo. I've been scared of horses all my life but there I was doing handstands in the saddle and riding two at once like water skis."

"That's a laugh." Ted swung back in from the kitchen, his voice a mumble around the cookie in his mouth. "Marcy's terrified of horses."

"I just told him that," she said.

"It's a good dream," I said.

"I had on this sequined leotard. And a rhinestone belt with a big buckle. I have no idea what it could mean."

Ted stood, chewing, behind the couch.

"Don't get her started," he said. "She took a class."

Marcy blushed and waved her hand in the air beside her ear, as if to consign the subject over her shoulder and into the past where it belonged.

The fire had burned to coals by the time we packed it in. Marcy walked me up to the guest room. To make sure I had everything I needed, she said. Ted was downstairs performing his nightly rounds—checking the locks, hitting the lights.

"I'm so glad you're here, Frank. He doesn't like to make a big deal out of it but family means the world to Ted." She swiped a strand of hair behind her ear. We were perched on opposite corners of the bed. "Ever since your mother died . . ." She dropped her eyes. "Your poor father . . ." Her voice trailed off again.

I would have been interested to hear whatever it was Marcy was having trouble putting into words but I didn't want to press. Those collarbones. Those slender wrists. I was happy to let her off the hook.

"I'm glad to be here," I said.

"I don't want you to think I'm a crazy person. That class I took, Ted makes it sound all new-agey but it wasn't. The Practical Meaning and Application of Dreams. That's what it was called. We only met one night a week."

She told me she'd seen a flyer for an adult outreach program at the community college up the road, told me the professor had a PhD from Brown.

"I don't think you're crazy," I said.

"I've always been interested in dreams," she said. "Ever since college. Freud and Jung and all that stuff. Every culture in the world puts stock in dreams."

"The chief nourishers of life's feast," I said.

Marcy raised her eyebrows.

"Shakespeare," I said. "*Macbeth*."

"You see," she said.

I heard Ted's footsteps on the stairs, then his voice in the twins' room, a low rumble, then his footsteps in the hall. Marcy pushed to her feet just as my brother came lurching in and flopped backward on the bed.

"The little sneaks were sleeping together." He rubbed his eyes with the heels of his hands. "Did I or did I not tell them to sleep in their own beds?"

Marcy stooped to read his watch. He was wearing one of those indestructible black titanium numbers that kept time in all twelve zones and was pressure-tested to something like ten thousand feet.

"It's Christmas," she said.

Ted said, "I don't see how that makes a difference."

I saw her consider whether or not to correct my brother's impression—her face was that unguarded—saw her decide against it. She looked at me instead.

"Is it true you never remember dreams?"

I might have told her that there were mornings when I came to feeling wistful and mislaid, with something nagging at me like a word on the tip of the tongue, but that wasn't the same thing as remembering.

"I think that's sad," she said.

When they were gone, I washed my face and gave my toothbrush a workout, then stripped to my boxers and hunched over my duffel for a minute, but I'd forgotten what I wanted. I knew as soon as I climbed into bed that I wouldn't be able to sleep but I lay there hoping for half an hour, scrolling through images like a microfiche machine (here was Dad dozed off in the shambles of his den and here was Ted with his hurt feelings and his eggnog and here was Marcy, too beautiful for community college, shooting her hand up when the teacher asked a question) and listening to those sounds that pass for silence in the middle of the night: the house creaking, branches ticking against the windows, warm air rushing in the ducts.

Eventually, I gave up on sleep and made my way down to the kitchen for macaroons and milk, which I consumed by the light from the open refrigerator. On the way back to bed, I noticed a pair of identical faces peering at me from the doorway of the twins' room.

"Hey, girls," I said.

"Uncle Frank?"

"It's me," I said. "It's late."

"Did Santa come?"

To say the twins spoke in unison isn't exactly right. It was more like bad looping in a movie or half-assed ESP. They spoke over and around each other, one of them rushing ahead or lagging behind, not always using the same words but arriving at more or less the same meaning every time. It's impossible to do justice to it on the page but believe me, some scientist somewhere could have done a study.

"Not yet," I said.

"Do we have to go back to bed?"

"He won't come if you're awake."

They looked at each other, then back at me.

"Will you stay with us until we fall asleep?"

"All right," I said.

I followed them into their room, watched, without remark, as they climbed into the same bed, a four-poster with a frilly canopy. I knew my brother would've wanted me to speak up but the scene was too lovely to disturb. There was an identical bed not six feet away, along with duplicate nightstands and chests of drawers and a table with matching ice cream parlor chairs, everything done in shades of white, each side of the room a moonlit reflection of the other. I wasn't sure what the twins expected, so I just tucked them in, then stood there looking out the window until I could see the first pale glimmer of dawn mirrored on the bay.

Picture me manning the video camera on Christmas morning while my brother led the twins on a pony ride around the yard. The ponies were black all over, speckled with white in places like somebody had flicked them with a paintbrush. The twins weren't so much riding as engaged in mounted hugs. Each had her arms wrapped around a pony's neck, her face pressed into a mane. Marcy was out there, too, warming her hands around a coffee mug. She was wearing a puffy white coat over her robe and her eyes were still bleary from sleep. Every time I put the camera on her, she ducked and waved me off but she looked great, like a team of hairdressers had devoted the predawn hours to styling her coiffure into a perfect balance between realistically disheveled and believably together. Maybe it was the camera but I kept feeling one step removed from everything or like all this was a set, the ponies and the girls and Ted, the bay behind them as bright and crinkled-looking in the sun as a sheet of foil. Neighbors popped out onto their porches to witness the happy commotion in my brother's yard. And Ted was really hamming it up. In his flannel pajamas and his duck boots and his parka, he strutted like the leader of a marching band.

When we were kids, Mom had a rule about opening one present, one person at time. We went around in a circle. It was meant to teach us a lesson in patience or something. But there was no such rule in my brother's house. They let the wrapping paper fly. I gave Ted *The Outlaw Josey Wales* on DVD, Marcy a porcelain compote I'd found in an antique store. They gave me a cashmere sweater and a set of barbecue tools. I refrained from mentioning that I didn't own a grill. I could see the ponies tied to a picnic table in the backyard, nipping at the meager grass that pushed up through the snow. At some point, Marcy produced a sausage and egg casserole which we ate while waiting for the twins to finish tearing into their gifts.

In the weeks leading up to Christmas, Ted had given me complicated instructions about shopping for the girls: It was absolutely necessary to give them separate presents, he said, never one big item to share, which apparently was a temptation with twins. It was vital that they conceive of themselves as individuals. It was also important, however, to give them exactly the same thing so there'd be no envy or hard feelings. I had settled on costume jewelry, matching sets of faux diamond chokers and tennis bracelets and clip-on earrings. They didn't seem particularly impressed but Marcy oohed and aahed to make me feel better.

"Tell Uncle Frank thank you."

"Thank you, Uncle Frank," they said and moved on to the next package in the pile.

Finally, we all gathered at a phone mounted on the kitchen wall to call the grandparents, Marcy's family first, then Dad. The twins held the phone between them and chattered about the ponies, then Marcy got on just long enough to wish Dad Merry Christmas. Ted was next. He hoisted himself onto the counter and swung his legs, heels thumping the cabinets while he talked. I leaned against the refrigerator waiting my turn. "Yeah," Ted said. "We've had a big time." He hopped down from the counter and started moving breakfast dishes into the washer, the phone pinned between his shoulder and his ear. "What about you?" He poured detergent and turned the dial, then stood at the pass-through listening with a hand bridged over his eyes. Marcy was in the living room now helping the twins into their new riding gear. It looked like some kind of festive bomb had gone off in there, shredded tissue and wrapping paper everywhere in sight. "I don't know." Ted listened again, then said, "I'm not sure that's the best idea, Dad. They're still pretty young. Here's Frank, OK?" He snapped his hand away from his brow like a salute and passed the phone to me.

"Ponies?" my father said when I picked up. "Lord."

He didn't sound drunk exactly but his voice was warm and slow in a way I recognized. The clock on the microwave said 10:08. Ever since I was a kid, Dad had maintained a policy about not drinking until after 5:00 but on special occasions, he allowed himself a Bloody Mary or two regardless of the hour.

"Did you have a nice morning?" I said.

"I spent a few hours with your mother. The cemetery looked like hell. Just because it's December doesn't mean they aren't obliged to provide an attractive resting place."

Everybody else had gone back outside for a last ride before someone from the farm came around to pick up the ponies. I could see them through the big windows in the living room, the girls arrayed like extras from *National Velvet,* waiting patiently while Ted and Marcy hashed something out. My brother frowned and shook his head.

I asked Dad if he'd opened his presents.

"Not yet."

"You should open your presents, Dad."

"I know," he said. "I will."

"There might be a pony in there for you."

"I'm too old for ponies. Can you return a pony? Can you take a pony back if it isn't what you wanted?"

"I have my doubts," I said.

While I watched, Marcy smiled too brightly at Ted, handed him a lead, lifted the twins one after the other onto a single pony's back, and I understood what they were hashing out. The twins wanted to ride double. My brother was against the idea but Marcy was ignoring him. She leaned against the rope, but the pony didn't budge. She stiffened, breathed deep, swiped the hair out of her face, said something to Ted without looking at him. Ted walked over and slapped the pony lightly on the rump. You could tell, even from a distance, that his effort was halfhearted, but the pony skittered forward a few steps like he'd been stung, then planted his hooves a moment before rearing his back end and jerking his legs out behind him like a bronco, sending both girls over his neck into the snow. All of this took place in seconds, not even long enough for the silence between Dad and me to get uncomfortable, but it seemed much longer than that and there was an instant, just before the twins were unseated, when they looked poised in time, wide-eyed and gape-mouthed, unsure but not yet afraid, as if on the verge of an epiphany. Then they were down and I could hear the muted sound of their crying and Ted and Marcy were swooping in to pick them up.

"I'm sorry, Dad. I have to go," I said and I hung up just as Ted and Marcy burst into the house, each holding a twin. As they passed, headed upstairs in a hurry, sobs trailing out behind them like fading sirens, Ted barked at me to "do something" with the ponies. I had no idea what that something might be but I was happy to make myself useful. The ponies lifted their heads at my approach, then flared their nostrils, simultaneously, and executed a pair of world-class, world-weary sighs. I had assumed that they were young (because of their stature, I guess) but now I wondered if my brother had procured a pair of old birthday party veterans or petting zoo retirees, nursing a lifetime of pony woes, fed up at last with children riding double.

Eventually, a woman from the farm showed up and Ted gave her an earful, featuring words like *negligence* and *liability*, which she heard without batting an eye. He mentioned nothing about getting his money back so I figured he was just venting. The woman was short and hippy with big forearms and a braid down to the middle of her spine. She seemed accustomed to ignoring yahoos like my brother. When he was finished, I helped her walk the ponies around to a trailer and she hauled them off into what was left of Christmas morning.

The twins were a little shaken up but nothing serious. I couldn't see a mark on them when Marcy brought them down. They were wearing red velvet dresses and patent leather shoes. All of a sudden we were running late for church. We slipped into Holy Innocents Episcopal after the readings but before the gospel, just in time to sing a few carols and hear the standard homily on the true meaning of Christmas. It was still cold out but it had warmed enough to get all the rain gutters in town ringing with snow melt. Bay Street was like a postcard, restaurants and galleries and boutiques, the whole world tinseled and garlanded for the holiday and more beautiful somehow for being deserted. But a moody fog had settled over us after the incident with the ponies and it failed to dissipate after church. Nobody said much in the car and everyone went their separate ways when we got home. The twins bolted to the playroom with a DVD and Ted shut himself up in his office and Marcy got busy preparing her Christmas spread.

I decided to take a walk. I hadn't been to church in a long time and I felt released after the service. Plus, I thought my brother's family could use some private time. The boardwalk spanned the shore from the Punta Clara Hotel to Zundel's Wharf, maybe three miles altogether. I set out in the direction of the hotel, hands in my pockets, chin tucked into the collar of my coat, waffling on the subject of my father. I couldn't make up my mind about dropping in on him tonight. The drinking didn't worry me as much as the fact that he was blowing Christmas off. I could picture his presents gathering dust in the foyer, bows wilting like old flowers. At the same time, I was flattered that my brother wanted me to stay, that it meant something to him, and I was pleased, secretly, shamefully, to be caught up in the middle of all this.

For most of its hundred some odd years, the Punta Clara Hotel had served as a kind of old-fashioned family resort (outdoor swimming pool, shuffleboard, croquet on the lawn), the sort of place where parents could turn the kids loose after dark without concern and soft-footed black waiters circled the dining room refilling cocktails without having to be told. There was music and dancing every night but only until ten o'clock, a famous Dixieland brunch on Sundays. In the last decade, however, the Punta Clara had been purchased by a conglomerate and converted into a spa/golfer's paradise. The original rooms had been retooled and they'd installed a massage facility where the band shell used to be and a former PGA champ had been retained to overhaul the links. Outside, the hotel maintained an air of vaguely decrepit glamour, crumbly bricks and Spanish moss drooping from the live oaks, but inside, you could just as easily have been in Ohio or Arizona. I wandered through the lobby and the bar and past the row of shops, all of it bright and bland as nickels, made a lap around the grounds, drifted down to the pier, its pennants aflutter, sailboat rigging chiming in the wind, then started back to Ted's. I'd been gone an hour. I hoped that was time enough to clear the air.

My brother was waiting in his boat when I returned. His face was red and his eyes were watery. I had the idea he'd been out there for a while. Twin Evinrude 150s burbled at the stern, billowing exhaust. He waved his arms over his head at my approach, as if trying to signal me from a great distance.

"Where you been?" he said. "We've only got a couple of hours til Marcy puts dinner on the table," and I wondered if, in my distraction last night, Ted had scheduled a boat ride for the two of us without my noticing. He pointed at a cleat on the corner of the wharf. "Get that line."

For twenty minutes, I was thoroughly preoccupied by the wind, lips numb, teeth chattering, the rest of me shivering under my coat. I was already chilled from the walk, had been looking forward to warming up by the fire, but now Ted was plowing across the bay at full throttle, ours the only boat in sight. I had no idea where he was taking me but, eventually, Middle Bay Light took shape in the distance, little more at first than a pencil smudge against the horizon but solidifying into itself faster than I would have thought possible. It looked more like somebody's crazy summer cottage than the standard New England version of a lighthouse. Hexagonal in shape, white with black shutters, warning lantern built right onto the roof. The whole business was raised on a web of pylons and guy wires and plopped down a mile from either shore. Ted cut the motor and we glided within thirty yards. By March, this place would be crawling with fishermen plumbing the depths for snapper or tourists out on a sightseeing trip from the Punta Clara, but at the moment, we shared it only with the gulls.

Ted opened a sliding panel in the console, came out with a sleeve of saltines and started crumbling crackers overboard. Within seconds, the air was aswarm with noisy birds, dozens of them, swooping in almost close enough to touch, beating the air with their wings. They dipped their beaks into the water, retreated with their spoils to the lighthouse, then lifted off once more to get back into the fray.

"I like it out here," Ted said.

He was hunting around in the console again. This time, he retrieved a silver flask. He sipped, handed it over. Brandy. I was glad to have it. My face felt like a mask of itself in the cold, unnatural and stiff. For a while, we just sat there drinking and baiting the gulls. Then Ted said, "I'm sorry about this morning." He was staring over his shoulder, away from me, in the direction of Mobile.

"For what?"

He shrugged. "I told Marcy riding double was a bad idea. The twins, they want to do everything together. Eat off the same plate and share the tub and sleep in the same bed. They talk at the same time. Have you noticed? Marcy thinks it's no big deal."

"Won't they grow out of that?" I said.

Ted looked at me like the last thing he needed was his little brother's opinion on childhood development. He sighed and rubbed his face with both hands, as if to wipe away ill feeling.

"Are you gonna stay the night?" he asked.

I took a drink and passed the flask. A lone seagull perched on the bow, watching us sidelong.

I said, "You know that wig Mom had? Long and red? The last one she bought, I think?"

Ted stopped the flask halfway to his lips, lowered it without drinking, let his hand rest on his thigh.

"What about it?"

"Dad still has it. On one of those mannequin heads. Right beside the bed."

"Here we go," Ted said.

"You don't think that's creepy?"

"Yes, Frank. Yes, it's creepy. That's exactly why he should be out here with us right now instead of holed up in that house. That's exactly why you should quit holding his hand. This is what I've been telling you."

"He drinks too much," I said.

Ted nodded like he was not surprised. "I tried to tell him it was a bad idea to retire. I told him a hundred times. Did he listen? Of course not. His wife was dead and his judgment was clouded. I understand that; I'm not an asshole. What I fail to understand is why my little brother won't help me help him."

"I don't think he likes me very much," I said.

Ted did a rankled furrow with his brow, then brought the flask up quickly to his lips and took a big drink and in a gasping, wheezy, angry voice said, "Oh, fuck you, Frank." If we'd been back at the house, I'm sure he would have stormed off, slammed a door on his way out, but out here, there was nothing but water on all sides. He worked the key in the ignition but the outboards had gotten cold while we fed the seagulls, didn't want to turn over. Ted cursed and jiggled the choke and the motors came coughing to life at last and he put us on a silent course toward home.

The house had undergone a transformation in my absence. The air smelled rich and warm with cooking. The living room had been detailed, all that wrapping paper and plastic packaging whisked out of sight, all those presents stowed. A new fire had been laid over last night's ashes. Marcy was putting the finishing touches on the table. There were flowers in complicated arrangements and flickering candles and wedding china and tasseled cords around our napkins. The silver gleamed. And Marcy—her hair was pulled back now, knotted at the nape of her neck with a velvet ribbon, and her face was flushed with kitchen warmth. The whole scene was straight out of my imagining of their lives. She looked up and smiled as we came in, both of us huffing into our hands and beating our arms against our sides. We'd hardly spoken since my brother turned the boat around.

"You boys wash up," she said.

Ten minutes later, dinner was served. Turkey and wild rice and salad and asparagus and corn pudding and buttery-looking rolls. Ted asked the twins to say a blessing and we all held hands and they launched without hesitation into a prayer they knew by heart, very Episcopal, exactly as subdued and gracious and lovely as the table.

"How do you tell them apart?" I said.

"They can hear," Ted said. "Don't talk about them like they're not in the room."

Marcy started, gave Ted a look, but he was spooning wild rice into his mouth and didn't meet her eyes. To me, she said, "It's not so hard. It was harder when they were little. We had to paint Colleen's fingernails. Her fingernails were small as lemon seeds."

The twins said, "I don't remember that."

"You were babies," Marcy said.

Ted let his spoon fall with a clatter. He wiped his mouth and pushed his chair back from the table and walked around behind the twins. "I'd like to conduct a little experiment," he said.

Marcy said, "What are you doing?"

"This'll be fun. On your feet, girls. Frank, you close your eyes."

He stared until I did as he instructed. I know how this will sound but in that moment, with my eyes closed, I had the sense that I could see my brother clearly. All he wanted was for me and Dad to come over here and poke around and find his life worthwhile, even if it wasn't as perfect as it looked. He wanted the present to get equal billing with the past. That seemed reasonable enough. But knowing this didn't change anything with Dad. In his eyes, I thought, Ted's life must have looked like proof that the world wasn't much affected by our mother's death, that her passage through time mattered less than it should have. What good was I between them? A few seconds later, Ted told me it was all right and I opened my eyes to find the twins stationed on either side of my brother. He had a hand on each blond head.

"Who's who?" he said.

I studied them for what felt like a long time, long enough for a blush to prickle up, but I couldn't make out a difference. Round cheeks, full lips, tapered chins, dainty ears, all identical, right down to the matching blue crescents under their eyes. I wondered if their fatigue was the result of ordinary Santa Claus anticipation or some more pressing and personal girlish concern.

Marcy touched my leg under the table.

"Why don't I guess instead," she said. "Hmmmm. Blond hair, blue eyes. You must be Lily?"

It was obvious, even to me, that she'd gotten the answer wrong on purpose, but the twins howled at her mistake, did a happy lap around my brother, rearranged themselves at his sides. "Do it again!" they chanted. "Do it again!" Ted was standing there with his arms crossed, looking at me like he'd made his point.

Marcy steered us back on course with small talk (the twins at their new school and Shakespeare Express and an interesting case my brother had been working on, involving a particular brand of hairspray that had a rare but real tendency to ignite if used in combination with a curling iron) and we made it through pecan pie without further incident. The twins were none the wiser, that I could tell, were even pleased by this curious interlude at their table and refused for the rest of the meal to answer to their right names.

Afterward, Marcy took the girls up for their bath and my brother got busy on the dishes. I offered to help but he said, "You're my guest." His tone was not entirely unfriendly, though I was pretty sure he wanted to be alone or at least that he didn't want to be alone with me. So I headed up to my room. It didn't take long to pack my duffel but when I was finished, I felt tired, heavy-limbed, short of breath. I stretched out on the bed, listened to water running in the pipes, the murmur of female voices down the hall, my brother clattering in the kitchen. For a while, I hoped that Ted would finish up and seek me out and we'd have one of his patented heart-to-hearts. He could go on about my lack of ambition and direction, my unwillingness to commit, whatever, and instead of tuning him out or changing the subject, I'd bob my head like he really had me pegged. But he found something else to do after the dishes. I picked up the phone beside the bed and dialed the number of my youth, intending to let Dad know I was coming. It rang for a long time, remote, inconsequential, then he answered and I snugged the receiver hard against my ear.

"Hey, Dad."

"Ted?"

"It's me," I said. "It's Frank."

"Hang on," he said.

There was rustling on the line and I pictured him patting his breast pocket for his glasses. I heard what sounded like a woman's voice on his end and for an instant, I thought maybe he'd patched things up with Madame Langlois, but the voice died out and I thought it was just TV, likely some no-nonsense anchorwoman on CNN, and I knew right then that I wasn't going home.

"What can I do for you?" he said.

"Nothing. Just checking in."

"I opened my presents," he said. "No ponies but thanks for the book." I'd given him a JFK biography. "And thank Ted and Marcy for the tie. And the DVD player. Which I'll never figure out."

"Maybe I can help with that," I said.

There came a tapping at the door and Marcy poked her head into the room. She apologized for interrupting, told me the girls wanted to say good night.

Dad said, "Was that your brother?"

"Marcy," I said. "Putting the girls to bed. Ted told me to tell you Merry Christmas, though. He said tell you Merry Christmas and he loves you."

"That reminds me," Dad said. "There's something I meant to tell you. I was gonna tell you this morning but you got off in such a rush." He coughed and cleared his throat. I could hear ice clinking in his glass. "Remember that little Graceland? There's a *For Sale* sign in the yard. Apparently, the husband got busted passing bad checks. The wife is moving back to Memphis. That's what the neighbors told me anyway."

"Elvis has left the building," I said.

Then we did our good-byes and I stood there for a minute with the phone still at my ear, a rushing on the line like the ocean in a seashell, before hanging up and making my way to the twins' room down the hall.

～

Marcy was still tucking them in. She slipped her arm into the crook of my elbow and steered me between the beds and gave me a look, half pleading, half amused. "Now listen, girls. Uncle Frank knows. He'll tell you it's better if you sleep in separate beds."

The twins were watching me, their faces sober but not entirely resigned. They each had an arm atop the blankets, an arm beneath, one right, one left, a perfect mirror image.

"Your mother's right," I said.

"Why?"

I looked at Marcy. Marcy shrugged.

"Where's Ted?" I said.

She jerked a thumb in the direction of the windows.

"He's been in already. You know Ted. He delivers his orders and expects to be obeyed."

After a moment, the twins said, "Why can't we sleep in the same bed?"

"There must be a good reason. I just can't think of it right now." I tried a goofy smile, the useless but lovable uncle. "Why do you want to?"

"I don't know," they said.

I walked over to the window. There was a light burning on the wharf and I could see Ted in his boat, just sitting there behind the wheel, breath puffing out of him like tiny smoke signals.

"Have you named the ponies yet?" I said, turning back to the twins.

They shook their heads.

I said, "You know your father and I are named after presidents. Theodore and Franklin Roosevelt. They were related somehow. Your grandfather, he admires them both. Despite the fact that Teddy was a Republican. Teddy bears are named after Teddy Roosevelt."

Marcy took my hand, linked our fingers. The twins said nothing in reply and who could blame them? Even I didn't know what I was talking about.

"I'm sorry," I said and I wondered how many times I'd uttered those words in my life and how many times you had to say a thing before it had no meaning anymore.

Marcy gave my hand a squeeze.

I said, "I couldn't tell you two apart."

They looked at me slyly for a moment. Then one said, "I'm Lily," and the other said, "I'm Colleen," and they were able to maintain their composure only for a second before collapsing into hysterics. They thrashed in their beds and kicked their feet under the covers and after a moment Marcy and I laughed with them.

"You think that's funny?" I said.

"Yes," they said.

I told them, "I do, too."

~

Ted didn't look up as I made my way out to the wharf but I know he heard me coming.

"Permission to board?" I asked.

He shrugged and I hopped into the boat and sat along the gunnel.

"You're still here," he said.

"I talked to Dad."

Ted made a noise in his throat. You couldn't see the city itself, the buildings and the houses and so on, but across the bay, Mobile pushed a dome of ambient light into the sky like a sci-fi movie force field.

"You know what he said to me this morning? He said I needed to bring the twins over to see Mom's grave."

I kept my mouth shut. I didn't know what Ted wanted me to say.

He cupped his hands over his head. "They haven't been since the funeral. They were babies then." He closed his eyes. "Did he sound all right?"

"He's fine," I said. "He told me to tell you that he loves you and Merry Christmas and everything."

"It's weird," he said. "I can go weeks without even remembering that Mom is dead. And then some little thing reminds me and I miss her and it hurts but it doesn't last for long." He pinched his nose against the cold and his voice went funny. "Do you miss her?"

"Sometimes," I said. "Right now."

After a moment, he said, "Do you believe in God?"

"Are you about to go evangelical on me?"

He dropped his hand and laughed softly, a little bitter, a little sad but nonetheless amused.

"I'm an Episcopalian, for Christ's sake."

"Then I don't know," I said.

He looked at me a second, seemed about to speak, then looked away. He crossed his arms and thrust his feet out. At bottom, I thought, his question had to do with Mom, whether or not she could see us right that minute and what she would think of us if she could. I had no answers, of course, nothing but platitudes regarding love and memory. I considered all the things I could tell my brother, Madame Langlois and miniature Graceland and how proud Dad was of him, and maybe I was being selfish, maybe I just wanted to keep those things for myself, but somehow none of it seemed right.

"You ever do any fishing on this boat?" I said.

He was a little reluctant at first but I prodded and Ted explained that he'd only had the boat a month but in the spring, when the reds were running, he didn't intend to miss a weekend. He showed me the loran and the live-bait well. For some reason, he cranked the motors and we sat there listening for a long time like they were playing a song he wanted me to hear.

That night, I woke desperate and panting and not at all sure where I was. The blinds were sort of half twisted shut, moonlight snaking in between the slats, casting unfamiliar shadows. There was something vaguely floral and cold-smelling in the air. I blinked and rubbed my eyes and one of the shadows moved and Marcy materialized like magic at the foot of the bed.

"I didn't mean to scare you," she said.

"What is it? Is something wrong?"

"No, no," she said. "I was just thinking. In class, we had to set an alarm at night so we could wake up in the middle of our dreams and write everything down before we forgot. I just thought, you know, maybe you might like to try."

I pushed up on my elbows. She was wearing gray silk pajamas, her hair held back with a terry-cloth headband. Moonlight. Silk. Her face exposed.

"I'm sorry," she said. "I shouldn't have."

"It's fine," I said.

"Do you remember anything?"

"Let's see." I reached for the lamp but Marcy said, "Leave it off. The dark helps sometimes."

I closed my eyes. My mind was empty but for the afterimage of her face, hazy and silver as a photographic negative. I didn't want to disappoint her.

"There were trees," I said. "Birds."

The mattress shifted with Marcy's weight. I opened my eyes and she was sitting there with her legs crossed, pinching her lower lip. "That's a start," she said. The next thing she said caught me off guard. She lay back on the bed and rolled onto her stomach and bent her knees so her feet were in the air. Her heels were white as ice.

"Would you mind if I put my head on your shoulder?"

I shook my head and she crawled toward me and rested her cheek upon my chest. She drew my arm around her like a shawl. It was her I'd smelled. Skin cream or hand lotion or something in her hair.

"Your brother's not so bad," she said.

I said, "I know."

"He loves you, you and your father."

"I know that, too."

"Do you have someone, Frank?" she said. "It makes me sad to think of you alone."

"I have someone," I said.

"Do you really? Who? Tell me what's her name."

"Louise Langlois," I said. "She's French."

"Ooh la la." Marcy wiggled at my side. "Tell me more."

"I'll tell you this much: She's an older woman."

"How much older?"

I said, "Thirty years," and Marcy gasped and slapped my stomach. "No," she said. "Really?"

"It's true."

"You're terrible," she said and I didn't know if she meant the age difference or if she knew that I was lying. "Don't let me fall asleep," she said and I told her I wouldn't but it wasn't long before I sensed her breathing even out, her body soften against me. I had no idea how she could sleep with my heart pounding beneath her ear. Against my will, an erection had perked up in my lap and I waited until it subsided before waking her. I didn't want to wake her up at all but I couldn't let my brother's wife pass the night with me in bed. I shook her gently and she blinked and pushed her fingers through her hair. "Oh," she said, in a voice filled up with wonder. "I dreamed I was in a caravan in the desert. Except instead of camels we had ponies. They had these chests of rare spices and jewels and magic carpets on their backs."

"You're making that up," I said.

"I'm not," she said. "I swear."

～

This would be a better story if I could report that I organized a reconciliation between my father and my brother. Maybe I convinced Ted to tag along when I went to look in on Dad and, because we were none of us bad men, all of us well intentioned, we put the last few months behind us and spent the day after Christmas pitching horseshoes and drinking beer. But that's not what happened. What happened was I overslept the next morning and stepped into my pants from the night before and pulled a T-shirt over my head and bumbled downstairs, hoping Ted and Marcy had left a little coffee in the pot. As I approached the kitchen, I heard Marcy's voice, hushed but intent, and I stopped shy of the door to listen.

"They're afraid," she said.

"And coddling them isn't going to help," Ted said. "In the long run coddling never did anybody any good."

"Just wait a day or two. It's my fault they're scared. You said riding double was a mistake. I know. But I don't want to rush them into anything. I don't want to make it worse. In a couple of days, they'll have forgotten about being scared."

"There's an old saying about this, Marcy."

"I know but—"

"It applies," Ted said.

"Yes but—"

"There has never been a more perfect application."

"Fine," Marcy said.

"I've already called the farm. They're expecting us at noon. The ponies will be saddled and all the twins will have to do is walk a couple of laps around the ring."

Marcy said, "I stopped arguing three sentences ago."

And I backpedaled as quietly as I could and tiptoed up to my room and brushed my teeth and slicked some water through my hair and collected my duffel bag, intending to make my exit as soon as I politely could. Likely Ted was right, I thought, but even so, I wasn't interested in bearing witness while the twins faced down their fear.

By ten o'clock, we were gathered around my Subaru. The scene was such a near approximation of my arrival I felt a wash of déjà vu. Marcy had the twins give me a hug good-bye and she kissed me on the ear and I shook my brother's hand. Then his new house was fading in the rearview mirror, the first Christmas of the new millennium already in the past. I crossed the bay on I-10, dipped under the river in the Bankhead Tunnel, reemerged on Water Street, Mobile rising around me like an ambush.

When school resumed after the holidays, I went back on the road with Shakespeare Express, first through Georgia, then a lap through Tennessee, then a few dates in Mississippi. At a military school in Pascagoula, I slipped midscene into Puck, when I was supposed to be doing Oberon, and on the ride home I couldn't quit thinking how sad it was all that poetry had blurred up in my mind, sadder still that no one but my scene partner noticed the mistake.

Near the end of March, on a beer run, I spotted Madame Langlois at Winn-Dixie with a man about her age. He had a goatee and walked with a limp. They were arguing over lamb chops. I ducked behind a freezer case to spy.

"*Non,*" Madame Langlois was saying. "Listen to me, Brock. The lamb, it must be simmered patiently in a dry red wine. This is not—how you say?—fast food."

Brock limped over to the butcher's counter and tapped a big class ring against the glass.

"Sounds like an awful lot of trouble when I've got a perfectly good grill collecting cobwebs in the carport."

Madame Langlois took his arm and drew him up and pecked his cheek. "You Americans," she said.

I hustled to the beer aisle and through the checkout line and beat it out of Winn-Dixie undetected. I had no idea what, if anything, my father had done to "fix it" with Madame Langlois, but I was glad for her, glad she'd found someone. Even so, seeing her like that had left me feeling at loose ends. On impulse, I drove over to Magnolia Cemetery, where I hopped the fence and toted the six-pack around looking for my mother's grave. Magnolia Cemetery covers about three hundred acres, however, and I got disoriented among the sarcophagi and the headstones. I wound up sipping beer at the base of a monument to a Confederate sailor named Hawkins Dent who met his end during the Battle of Mobile Bay.

What else? I took Dad out for a burger now and then or went over to his place to run a load of laundry if Lucious Son or Chloe Jones had the machine in use at Mrs. Mauldin's. While we waited, he'd drink scotch and whip me at chess or backgammon or whatever. Shakespeare Express zipped through the Florida panhandle. Ted and Marcy invited me to dinner a couple of times and once Marcy arranged for a part-time yoga instructor friend of hers to join us. This woman was so flexible she could bend all the way over backward and look out at you between her knees. She showed us after dessert. Ted gave me a bug-eyed, hubba-hubba smirk but the truth is she freaked me out.

One night, late, Lucious Son knocked on my door. Despite the martial arts and the weed peddling, he was generally a quiet neighbor, kept to himself, early

to bed and rise, maintained a strictly regimented sched-
ule of workouts and meditation. I was surprised by the
hour of his visit.

"I saw your light was on," he said. "I thought
you might gimme a little taste."

He was wearing a yellow gi with a red monkey
on the back. I waved him toward the desk chair but
Lucious kept his feet. I could hear rain on the roof and
on the trees, cars hissing by on Dauphin Street.

After a moment, I said, "Tis all men's office to
speak patience / To those that wring under the load of
sorrow / But no man's virtue nor sufficiency / To be
so moral when he shall endure the like himself."

Lucious shrugged and looked around. I figured
he was in the mood for something more upbeat.

"Is something wrong?" I said.

He shook his head. "Not with me. But you been
moping around here like somebody died."

And all of a sudden I was afraid that I would cry.
I blinked and sucked air over my teeth. I didn't know
what was going on but I didn't want to cry in front of
Lucious. I gripped the back of my desk chair. I kept
my eyes fixed on the floor.

"It's been a weird little while," I said.

Lucious said, "You should fast."

Maybe it was the utter out-of-the-blue-ness of
his proposal but as quickly as that rush of emotion had

bubbled up, it began to subside, drawn off into nothing like water down a drain.

"You think I should quit eating?"

"Narrows the focus, man. Your body understands what it needs. You just have to know how to ask."

"I'll keep that in mind," I said.

"That or I could get you stoned."

I said, "Some other night."

He cupped his hands and bowed, one corner of his mouth drawn up into what might have been a smile, then pulled the door shut as he backed into the hall.

In May, the twins turned five years old. They had a party at their house, pony rides and presents and other kids from their school. To my surprise, Dad agreed to let me drive him over. He marveled at my brother's house, roamed through the rooms, trailing his fingers along the walls as if he needed to touch something solid to remind himself that it was real. At first he and Ted were a little awkward together but I saw them slip away from the party at one point and sneak down to the wharf and I wondered why the holiday season had seemed so fraught when we were in the middle of it and then I thought it seemed that way because it was. Just because time and circumstance had conspired to smooth things over after the fact didn't change the way anybody felt at the time. Or that everything might have turned out differently if each of us hadn't played our roles exactly as we did.

Eventually, Marcy spotted me sitting alone at the picnic table. She walked over and sat beside me and looked where I was looking. Ted was demonstrating the live-bait well for Dad.

"Does that make you happy?" Marcy asked.

I told her, "Yes."

She looked at me slyly for a second, then took my hand and said, "Come with me, young man. There's someone I want you to meet."

I let her tug me to my feet and lead me into the kitchen, where a woman with shortish, curlyish, brown-ish hair was poking candles into a pair of matching birthday cakes. She was wearing a traditional white chef's coat with plastic flip-flops and faded jeans. On the counter beside the cake was her chef's hat, the top caved in like a failed soufflé.

"Frank," Marcy said. "This is Dori Vine. Dori's son is in school with the twins."

"Oh," I said.

"I'm divorced." She poked the chef's hat out and set it lightly atop her head. "Almost six months. Marcy thinks you should be my rebound guy."

Marcy socked her in the arm and said, "In addition to being tactless, Dori owns a bakery in Point

Clear." She raised up on her toes and whispered, "She thinks you're cute," into my ear, her breath making my skin go goose-pimply and warm.

I liked Dori well enough and her son turned out to be a nice kid and they both liked me, I think, but we barely got off the ground. Two dates: one dinner, just the two of us, and a trip to the Exploreum with her son. That was it, before Dori decided she wasn't ready to move on. I was disappointed at first but that wore off and I felt oddly heartened for the effort.

After that, Shakespeare Express went back on hiatus for the summer and I did *The Beautiful People* at The Playhouse and right when we were gearing up again for the fall, I got a phone call from the principal at my old high school. It seemed the regular drama teacher, one Minerva Trout, was on maternity leave for the semester and her original replacement had pulled out at the last minute and would I be interested in filling in? I didn't have to think about it long. By November, Minerva Trout had decided that she loved motherhood more than teaching, and I've been filling in ever since. I have a little office behind the auditorium and the students call me "Mr. Posey" and they're game enough on stage if not exactly brimming with talent. Just last week, Ted and Marcy accompanied Dad to our production of *Romeo and Juliet*.

Unabridged. Every beautiful word. I started this account as a play, in fact, hoping my students would be willing to put it on. It became clear after a while, however, that I had no third act, that our story had no clear-cut resolution and likely never would, that whatever we had gained, whatever accommodations we had reached, something was lost as well, some opportunity missed, perhaps, though the nature of that something is hazy to me even now. So here I am with you, dear reader, weary and unshaved but narrating for us Poseys as honestly as I can.

Love at the End
of the Year

....

The story ends. It was written for several reasons. Nine of them are secrets. The tenth is that one should never cease considering human love, which remains as grisly and golden as ever, no matter what is tattooed upon the warm, tympanic page.

—Donald Barthelme,
"Rebecca"

Katie

The Butters, Katie and Hugh, were stopped at the intersection of Cottage Hill and Cummerbund, lost, late for the Marchands' New Year's Eve party, when Katie decided to leave her husband. At that precise moment, Hugh was craning to look over his shoulder, headlights reflecting on his glasses. He faced front just as the light was changing, wiped the corners of his mouth, eased them uncertainly into traffic. Her husband, Katie knew, hated to be lost.

"I'm all turned around," he said. "What was that last street? Did you notice the sign?"

Katie shook her head.

"What?"

"No," she said.

"I'm trying to watch the road," Hugh said. "I can't watch you and the road at the same time. Audible responses, OK. I'd be grateful for a little help here, Katie."

Katie nodded, caught herself, cleared her throat.

"What street are we looking for?"

"Bow tie Lane."

"I'm leaving you," she said.

Right away, she wished she hadn't spoken. The patent symbolism of the occasion (new year, new life) hadn't occurred to her until that moment. It embarrassed her somehow, made her feel like a cliché. The unhappy housewife. She had spoken on impulse, on the strength of her emotion, but the truth was she couldn't have put to words the way she felt. Hugh leaned forward now, shut both the radio and the heater off. Cold and quiet seeped into the car like the very gist of winter.

"Point taken," Hugh said. "I shouldn't have snapped. But you know I hate being lost. You know how I get. No need to go all dramatic on me."

What Katie felt, more than anything, was relief. Her pronouncement had been erased, her unhappiness reduced to the product of a squabble, not uncommon even in a healthy marriage, easily repaired. She thought of the children (Evan, twelve; Nicole, eight) at home with Miss Anita. Tonight they would eat too much pizza and drink too much Coke and stay up past their bedtime, rare pleasures. How naturally happiness came to children.

"Katie?"

His voice surprised her.

"It's all right," she said.

"To top it off we're late. Forty minutes. I hate being late almost as much as I hate being lost."

"They'll understand."

"That's beside the point," Hugh said.

Evan

Evan Butter found hotbush.com on the Internet the day after Christmas. He'd talked his parents into getting him a computer and an online hookup for his room. Schoolwork, he said. It's the only thing I want this year, he said, hinting that if there wasn't a computer under the tree they'd have a deeply unhappy twelve-year-old on their hands. He knew they remembered how he'd sulked two years ago when they got him a three-speed instead of the mountain bike he asked for. He'd memorized his father's American Express number and had been downloading naked pictures of a woman named Veronica ever since (Veronica on a pool table, Veronica emerging from a hot tub, Veronica doubled over and mugging for the camera through her legs).

There were other women on the site (petite Autumn, busty Desiree, long-legged Lorelei) and there were other sites (bigsluts.com; beavershot.com), but he was faithful to Veronica. She reminded him of a girl named Lulu Fountain who went to his school and had acquired both breasts and braces the previous summer. She sat in the next desk over from his in Ms. Hempel's

English class, smelled faintly of maple syrup. Just before the holidays, he'd been flipping through his yearbook and come across her picture and circled it in red ink. The picture had been taken before the braces so he sketched them in across her smile. She hardly ever smiled like that anymore, her whole face in it. The emphasis in her features had shifted since the summer. Now she kept her mouth pinched shut, her eyes open wide like she was constantly in the process of being startled. He looked at her picture for a long time. Then he added a mustache and horns. If asked, he would have been hard pressed to explain what exactly Veronica and Lulu Fountain had in common beyond the most rudimentary physical similarities: brown hair, brown eyes. There was, however, a barely perceptible look of amazement in Veronica's features, as if she was surprised to find herself naked except for hip-high leather boots, the whole world looking on.

Tonight, his mom and dad were off somewhere at a party. He and his little sister, Nicole, were under Miss Anita's care. Miss Anita was the housekeeper. She was old and black and could be counted on to have no plans for New Year's Eve. She had children of her own (now and then, Evan heard his mother asking her about them) but they were grown, didn't need looking after anymore. Right now, Miss Anita was watching TV in the living room with Nicole, one of the New Year's countdown shows. Evan could hear music drifting up the stairs and under his locked door. He'd been masturbating pretty much nonstop since dinner. He was a little sore and more than a little bored but refused to admit it to himself. It didn't seem possible that such a wonder as Veronica could ever lose her charm.

Lulu

Lulu Fountain believed absolutely in the thunderbolt of love, as observed on the Turner Classic Movie Channel and in the novels of Jane Austen, believed that any action taken in its service could not possibly be wrong. Which was why she was trying not to feel guilty for running away from home this very night to live her life with a boy named Ike Tiptoe. Which was also why she was disappointed Ike had brought her, as usual, out to Illumination Meadows. There was nothing so wrong with the place itself. Illumination Meadows was an abandoned development out by the airport, lots staked off, foundations poured, the houses framed but unfinished, plastic sheeting tacked up to protect exposed drywall from the weather. It would have been plenty romantic if it was just the two of them, Ike and Lulu, tucked away in a half-built house, huddled together on New Year's Eve, but Illumination Meadows was where Ike and his friends liked to hide out from the world. Even now, even with Ike's hot mouth on her right ear, she could hear them downstairs, Ollie and Myrtle and Mary Lee and the two Neals, popping beer can tabs, laughing stoned laughs, scanning stations on the portable radio, and Lulu wanted more than anything for her and Ike to be alone.

Ike Tiptoe was seventeen, four years her senior. She'd met him at a football game. Lulu went to Immaculate Conception Middle. Ike went to Bishop O'Dell High, where all the kids from the parish schools around Mobile wound up eventually. Lulu's pep squad had been honored with an invitation to participate in the halftime show at Bishop O'Dell's homecoming and Ike approached her in the third quarter and she loved him right away, which was how she knew her love was true, his mismatched eyes (one hazel, the other blue) and how thin he was under his coat. In her daydreams, Lulu saw herself lithe and graceful (precisely the reason she'd been taking ballet for the past six years) with a kind of hard-to-put-your-finger-on appeal, but in the mirror she was plain as pocket lint, with her braces and her freckles and her brown, nothing special hair. Even her dance instructor, Mrs. Settle-Kidd, had told her that, while she was happy to have Lulu in the class, she was too "flat-footed," too "cumbersome of bone," to have a future in ballet. But Ike: From that first moment, it was as if he perceived Lulu as she imagined herself, not as she was.

"You look like that girl," he'd said. "That actress. She was in that movie in New York where she worked for a magazine and her mother had cancer. She used to be in that show about hairdressers."

Lulu knew exactly who he meant.

Stella

Here's how New Year's Eve kicked off for Stella Fountain:

First, she arrived home from work to find an eviction notice tacked to the door of her apartment. This was a nice building, an old hotel reclaimed, high ceilings, exposed brick, part of the city's effort to gentrify downtown, not the sort of place where evictions were run-of-the-mill. But she'd buzzed a burglar in last week. It was a Tuesday evening and Lulu was due home from ballet any minute (somebody else's mother brought her home on Tuesdays) and Stella always let her up without checking the intercom. The burglar made off with just over $6,000 worth of property, none of it Stella's, which made for plenty of hard feelings, she was sure. Because she refused to make restitution (it could've happened to anybody was how she saw it), the tenant council decided it was best for everyone if she found other accommodations.

Then she read the letter her daughter, Lulu, thirteen, had left on the dining room table. *Dear Bitch,* it began, and went on to list the various cruelties and indignities Stella had perpetrated on her poor child over the years, chief among which was the fact that Stella had forbidden Lulu to go on a car date that very evening with a high school boy named Ike Tiptoe. Consequently, Lulu had decided to live her own life, the letter said. She was practically a woman. Exclamation point. She could make her own decisions. Exclamation point. She didn't need a mother. Exclamation point. She could look after herself. Double exclamation point. *Sincerely, Lulu.*

Stella fixed a gin and tonic and sat on the couch waiting to cry but nothing happened so she called her ex-husband on his cell phone.

"What's up?" he said. "I'm in the car."

Stella had been divorced for almost four years. It had been an amicable proceeding. Irreconcilable differences were cited. Her husband, Boyd, had ceded custody to Stella without a fight, agreed to pay a generous percentage of his earnings in child support and handed it over each month without incident or complaint. For Lulu's sake, Stella had kept her married name. She and Boyd had managed to stay friends. Lunch now and then. Parent-teacher conferences. Lulu's ballet recitals. They still did holidays as a family. Together, they even took Lulu on a trip to see *Swan Lake* at the Kennedy Center last year. When she let herself think about it, Stella couldn't help concluding that their relationship was better now than ever.

There were nights when she couldn't quite recall the reasons her marriage had dissolved.

"Lulu hates me," Stella said. The sound of his voice had triggered her tears and she fought to blink them back. "She's run away from home. She left a note."

"She doesn't hate you, honey. I'm sure this is nothing, OK. Lulu's just acting out." There was a burst of static. "—what teenage girls do. They rebel against their mothers. Tell me what the letter said."

"It said she hates me."

Boyd asked her, "What else? There must be something."

"This boy, Ike Tiptoe. He's sixteen," Stella said. "I wouldn't let him take Lulu out in his car."

"That's good. You did the right thing, honey. Here's an idea: Why don't you try calling his parents. Maybe they know what's what."

"Would you come over?" Stella said.

"Stella, honey, I'm on the interstate right now. I'm on my way someplace."

"Please," she said.

There was a crackly pause. She knew it was just the connection but it was hard not to hear impatience in the sound.

"All right," Boyd said. "I'll be right there."

Stella sipped her drink, let the ice click against her teeth, imagined Boyd hunched up in his Mercedes.

He drove with his seat too close to the wheel for a man his size. She considered mentioning the eviction notice but decided it would sound too much like a plea for sympathy. She hadn't told him about the burglar. She worried it would make her seem helpless. She didn't want the man she'd once married to think of her that way.

Katie

The Marchands were friends from early in the Butters' marriage. They had lived in a neighborhood thick with smaller, older homes: wood floors, chipped paint, tidy lawns. Everyone was young, just getting started. Mark and Lauren Killibrew, Brett and Astrid Watts, Lee and Donna Mason. Katie was pregnant with Evan when they bought the house, with Nicole when they put it up for sale. They'd all moved on since then, some to bigger and better lives, some, like Boyd and Stella Fountain, sundered from them by divorce. They saw each other socially maybe once a year, usually at the Marchands' New Year's Eve soiree, made promises to spend more time together in the future, never did. The Marchands were the last to leave the neighborhood. Paul was a professor of mathematics, his rise in the world a little slower than the other husbands. The party was at their new house.

Somehow, almost as soon as they arrived, Katie got herself cornered by a stranger, a colleague of Paul Marchand's. His name, she thought, was Urqhardt. He was midforties, small (the top of his head barely reached the tip of Katie's nose) and he wore his hair too long for a man his age, past his collar. He was telling her that his apartment had been robbed last week.

"It was the strangest thing," he said. "We came home from the movies and we knew right away that something was weird. We didn't realize that we'd been robbed, of course. I mean, he didn't tear the place up or anything. There was nothing obviously different, understand. It was like this presence in the room."

"We?"

"My partner and me."

He pointed at a man standing by the fireplace with his elbow on the mantel. He was younger than Urqhardt by at least fifteen years, probably more. He dressed like a gay man. His clothes were stylish but too tight. Katie wouldn't have been surprised if he was Urqhardt's student. Other guests floated by, their heads like balloons passing through Katie's line of sight. Music. Voices. Closer, perched on the arm of the couch, was Hugh. He was talking to Haley Marchand.

"That's Kevin," Urqhardt said. He waved but Kevin didn't see him. "Anyhow, he only took little things. My pocket watch and Kevin's diamond studs, stuff like that, but we knew intuitively that our home had been invaded. I don't need to tell you I've been having nightmares ever since."

"How was the movie?" Katie asked.

Urqhardt blinked at her, smiled a close-lipped smile, as if she'd told a joke he didn't get. She realized, too late, that she'd been rude. She hadn't meant to be rude. The question had simply popped out of her mouth. She was intrigued, to tell the truth. That kind of dreadful intuition sounded awfully familiar.

"Not good," he said after a moment.

He drained his chardonnay, wagged the empty glass, a parting gesture, an irked farewell. She watched him drift over to the bar, then drift away, his glass refilled, watched him circle through the party, headed for the sunporch, describing a perfect arc as far as possible from Katie.

When she looked away, Katie was washed with a nervous, untethered feeling. Here she was alone in a roomful of people. Normally, she would have attached herself to Hugh, but after what she'd said, after what she told him in the car . . . It didn't matter that he misunderstood. Earlier that evening, she'd asked Hugh if he thought she'd gotten old and he told her she looked great in such an absent way that the hair on the back of her neck stood up like he'd said something spooky. Hugh had been picking lint off of his jacket at the time. At the moment, he was engrossed with Haley Marchand. He'd always had a crush on Haley, she thought. Nothing serious. Haley was pretty enough, different enough from Katie, that Hugh wanted her to be impressed with him. Right this minute, he was probably letting her know, without actually saying the words aloud, how much more money there was to be made in headhunting (Hugh owned his own headhunting outfit) than in the education game. Once, in the old neighborhood, Hugh had gotten drunk at a cookout in somebody's backyard and serenaded Haley with a medley of Beach Boys songs.

Miss Anita

Miss Anita knew exactly what was going on up in that boy's room. She had three sons of her own. She was remembering an April Thursday, barely a month after her husband died, when she'd gone back to her oldest's room to flip the mattress and found a sheaf of dirty magazines. Her first thought was what kind of stupid son had she raised to hide his dirty magazines in the bed. She wanted to roll them up and beat him like a dog. Her second thought, upon closer inspection, was that all the women in the dirty magazines were white. Weren't there any dirty magazines for black people? Her third thought, the one that made her bones feel soft and dropped her to her knees, was that her husband was gone and he wasn't coming back and she would have to sort this out alone. She shut her eyes and clasped her hands and asked Jesus what she should do.

"Don't do anything," He replied.

"What's that?"

"Leave the magazines where you found them and never speak of this to your son."

He sounded similar to but not exactly like the young lawyer on her favorite TV show.

"Is this a test?" she asked.

"Now is a time to count your blessings."

Miss Anita kept on praying and praying but Jesus did not speak again. After a while, after she'd gotten past her anger and confusion, she began to see the wisdom in His guidance. Her sons were healthy. The house was paid for. She had plenty of work. And she'd known love. That was something.

Now, sixteen years had passed and her boys were married off and raising children of their own. She had two miniatures of Peppermint Schnapps in her belly right this minute and she was feeling warm and slow and there were ten more in her purse. There was still plenty to be grateful for. The little girl, Nicole, was sitting beside her on the couch with her toes tucked under Miss Anita's thigh, and the boy, Evan, was doing what he was doing up in his room. She felt a pang of affection for them both, for being young and knowing nothing of the world. She hated to bother the boy but he'd been up there for hours and she was thinking she should at least let him know he was welcome to join them anytime. So she stepped into her slippers and creaked up to his room. The door was locked, which came as no surprise. She couldn't help teasing him a little. She rattled the knob.

"Whachu doing in there you need to lock a body out?"

No answer, but she could hear a frantic ticking sound.

"Boy?" she said.

"What?" His voice was high-pitched and constricted. "I'm not doing anything."

"You just sitting in there, hunh? All quiet? You just looking at the wall?"

"I'm playing a computer game," he said. "It's *Lucifer's Gate*."

"Lucifer," she said and she covered her mouth to keep from laughing. "Well, why not give old Lucifer a rest and come watch TV with your sister. We gone pop some popcorn in a minute."

"No thanks," he said.

Miss Anita said, "Un-hunh."

Lulu

She was wearing these low-slung jeans that exposed
the waistband of her thong and this black sweater that
showed off her belly-button ring and she was seriously
cold. Even with Ike all over her. Even with her blood
running crazy in her veins. They were making out
on the bench seat of a pickup truck, all musty-rusty
smelling and ripped in places and damp from a thousand rains. Ike and his friends cruised neighborhoods
after school looking for cast-off furniture: an old futon,
cracked-up box springs, this bench seat, a broken
La-Z-Boy, permanently reclined, which they set up
in the house as if they owned the place. Which they
sort of did. Ike's friend, Ollie, it was his father who
had bankrolled the development until the IRS came
calling for reasons not even Ollie could explain and
his father had to put everything on hold.

Three times before, Lulu had sneaked out of the
apartment after her mother had gone to sleep and Ike
had picked her up at the corner and brought her out
here with his friends and each time, they'd socialized
a minute, had a beer, smoked a little, then headed upstairs. Lulu had it in mind that this night would be

different. It was New Year's Eve after all, the perfect time for new beginnings, and she was in love. Which was why she'd made the mistake of telling her mother about Ike. Even her mother, who was divorced, who had only failed at love, even her mother, thought Lulu, had to respect the mysteries of the heart. She'd asked her mother for permission to go out with Ike this time, instead of slinking into the night. Her mother had, of course, refused. Lulu was too young and Ike was too old and there would be time enough for dating when she was in high school. Lulu cried and cried. Then she realized that, if you looked at it in the right light, her mother's pigheadedness was kind of perfect. Forbidden love was surely more meaningful than any love that received her mother's blessing. And this gave her an opportunity to prove to Ike just how enormous was her commitment. She hadn't told him yet that she'd run away or about the brutal but honest letter she had left for her mother to find. She clutched the secret close to her heart as if it helped to keep her warm.

One of the things she wanted to be different was this, right now, Ike mashing his tongue into her mouth, running his fingers up the inside of her thigh. It wasn't that she minded making out with him. Not at all. She understood that passion was an essential component of love and Ike made her, no doubt, all buttery inside. But tonight was "special." Even if Ike didn't know it yet. If he loved her (and she believed him when he said the words), shouldn't he have somehow sensed the monumental nature of the occasion? She wasn't entirely sure what she wanted from him, only that she wanted some kind of symbol, something deep and true to etch the night permanently in time.

"Ike," she said. "Wait a minute. Ike."

He was kissing her neck when she pushed him away, came up with her confirmation cross in his mouth, the chain dangling from between his lips. He was breathing hard, his eyes dopey and lost, his right hand on her left breast, under her shirt but on the outside of her bra.

"What?" His voice was a mumble around the cross and his hair was all messed up. He was the most beautiful thing she'd ever seen.

"Nothing," Lulu said and just like that he was kissing her again, his lips on hers a moment, long enough to pass her the cross (she felt it tick against her teeth), then her earlobe, then her neck again, his fingers fumbling now with the button of her jeans. Without really thinking about it, without either of them much noticing, she moved his hand to her hip, where it would begin its persistent crawl back toward her lap. The chain of her cross snagged on her braces but after a panicky few seconds, she was able to work it loose with her tongue.

Stella

On TV, the police always required a twenty-four-hour waiting period before filing a missing persons report. Stella didn't think she could wait a full twenty-four hours, but neither did she want to make a nuisance of herself. She decided she'd contact the authorities if she hadn't heard anything by midnight. It was 9:16 right now. She carried her second gin and tonic into Lulu's room, poked around in the closet, the desk, the nightstand, looking for a diary or letters from Ike Tiptoe, anything that might offer a clue to her daughter's whereabouts. Nothing. She picked up Lulu's phone, rang Information. There was only one Tiptoe (first name Roland) but the number was unlisted.

She dialed Lulu's friends, most of whom were out, put on a chatty voice for their mothers, tried to gather information without revealing the circumstances for her call, but nobody had seen or heard from Lulu.

She flopped back on Lulu's bed. Above her, tacked to the ceiling, was a poster of a bare-chested man in flesh-colored dancer's tights. His bulge was huge, had to be fake. She wondered how long it had been hanging there, how such a thing had escaped her attention.

Probably Boyd was right, she thought, this was nothing more than theater, a tantrum, but that didn't stop her insides from knotting up. She was on her third gin and tonic when the door buzzer sounded. It was Boyd's voice on the intercom, and Stella went all wobbly with relief.

"We got evicted," she blurted the instant she saw his face. She proceeded to dissolve into his arms, to loose her pent-up tears. "It's because of the burglar. I buzzed a burglar up last week. He hardly stole anything. The Groomes' silver and Professor Urqhardt's pocket watch and Mrs. Ripley's . . . that thing, you know, it's like what Miss America wears."

"Tiara?"

"That's right," she said. "Tiara."

Boyd said, "I'm not following."

Stella pushed away, thrust the letter and the notice into his hands (she'd let him sort it out himself), then sagged onto the couch to finish crying. Even in the moment, she was embarrassed by her behavior. In her regular life, Stella was plenty competent. In addition to raising a teenage daughter, she ran an antiques place on Upham Street, managed three employees, traveled to markets all over the country when Boyd was keeping Lulu, haggled dealers down to bare-bones prices. She hardly needed Boyd's alimony anymore. But there was tremendous comfort in letting herself go like this, in letting someone else worry about her problems. Especially Boyd. Whom she trusted. Who took great pride in his talent for crisis resolution. Boyd made his living in maritime law. Inside of twenty minutes, in the time it took Stella to collect herself, not only had he tracked down Luther Crews, president of the tenants' council, not only had he wrangled an extension on Stella's lease, pending settlement, but he'd somehow charmed an Information operator into the address for the only Tiptoe in the city.

Esmerelda

Two things were happening to Esmerelda Daza that had never happened in her life. She was waiting for a blind date. That was one thing. Worse than that, he was more than an hour late and she was beginning to fear he wasn't coming at all. That was the second thing. Bert, his name was. Or Hoyt. A silly, American name. Her feelings on the subject were somehow compounded by the fact that she was having a conversation with a gay man. He was going on about his apartment, a robbery last week, but she wasn't really listening.

Esmerelda was thirty-eight years old but from the right distance and in the right light she looked ten years younger. Dark hair, dark eyes. Her neck and legs were long and thin. Even now, she could feel other women's husbands pausing to drink her in. The only man in the room who wasn't impressed was the one monopolizing her company right this minute.

"I still don't feel safe in the apartment." He palmed his brow, as if checking his temperature, then his cheek, then the back of his neck. "The robbery, it changed something. I've tried to hash it out with Kevin but neither of us can put it into words."

Esmerelda nodded and smiled, lips just slightly parted, eyes narrowed to slits, the smile she generally reserved for letting a man know that she would sleep with him. But of course this man didn't notice.

"We've been together for eight months now," he was saying. "He moved in just before Halloween and it's been great, it really has, until the robbery, but now I can't stop feeling afraid."

"Before his death, Esmerelda's father had owned a company that shipped supplies to offshore oil rigs. He had offices on five continents and as a result, Esmerelda had known men from every culture in the world. In the past two decades, she had received eleven marriage proposals, all of which she'd refused for what seemed like good reasons at the time."

"Do you know what I mean?" the gay man said.

Occasionally, Esmerelda played doubles with a group of women here in town, and one of them was Haley Marchand. They were chatting over bottled water after a match last month when Haley began describing this man whose name Esmerelda couldn't remember even now, this lawyer, an old friend. Haley had run into him recently and he'd seemed so alone and he had no plans for New Year's Eve. Did Esmerelda?

What surprised her even more than Haley's presumptuousness was that she found herself intrigued. When had she reached the point in her life that she would consider such a thing?

She noticed, then, that the gay man was watching her expectantly, searching her eyes, waiting, it seemed, for her to speak. She touched her throat.

"I'm sorry," she said. "Are you asking if I have ever been afraid?"

Katie

Hugh was leaning into the open refrigerator, one hand on the top of the door, the other braced on his knee. Katie crept up behind him and stood there for a moment, watched him swiveling his backside in time to the music in the other room.

"Boo," she said.

Hugh started, clutched his chest in mock alarm.

"I'm looking for prosciutto," he said. "Haley sent me. Except there's no prosciutto in here that I can see."

He stepped aside to let Katie have a look. Amidst the standard refrigerator clutter, she saw a single can of beer tucked into the corner. She took it out and popped the top. The kitchen was a mess, the counter littered with empty serving dishes and discarded paper plates and plastic martini glasses with lipstick on the rims. Katie resisted the urge to tidy up a little. The refrigerator breathed cold air against her legs.

"Nope. No prosciutto."

"You know there's beer in the dining room. Where they've got the bar. Imports. Bottles."

"This is what I want," she said.

There were swinging doors at either end of the kitchen. One led into the dining room, the other to a sunporch. She spotted Urqhardt on the sunporch. He was talking to a Latin-looking woman in a floor-length skirt, his face earnest, his eyes intent, and Katie wondered if he was telling her about the robbery, that invasive presence. She wished she had the woman's legs. Hugh ran his hand down her arm, closed his fingers on her wrist, let her go. She could see the children in his face, Evan's sleepy-looking eyes, the shape of Nicole's mouth. She must have loved him sometime. She remembered this strange moment on her wedding day, maybe an hour before the ceremony. She was gazing at herself in the mirror and saw, suddenly, a dark shape behind her in the reflection. She whirled to face it but the room was empty. Then the vows, the champagne, the rice. Then the whole rest of her life.

"Do you ever see Boyd Fountain anymore?" she asked.

Hugh cocked his head. "I don't know. I mean, I bump into him sometimes. But not really, no. Not to speak of."

"What about Stella?"

"No," he said. "Why?"

"I'm leaving you," she said.

Hugh rolled his eyes. He smiled.

"Because I haven't paid you enough attention? It's a party, Katie. That's what you do at parties—mingle." Katie could feel the force of her words evaporating as he spoke. "Tell you what. Let me track Haley down, let her know she's out of ham, then we'll find a quiet spot. We'll talk." He brushed his lips against her brow, used his body to back her up so he could shut the refrigerator door.

Urqhardt

Urqhardt waited in plain sight until Kevin noticed he was alone. He watched Kevin separate himself from a conversation with a pair of unmistakably straight men. They were sporting holiday attire. Snowflake sweater. Reindeer tie. Gay men do not do seasonal themes. Kevin crossed the room with purpose, kissed Urqhardt on the ear.

"I can't tell you how interesting all this is," he said and Urqhardt was surprised by the real enthusiasm in his voice.

He'd debated long and hard about bringing Kevin to the party. Kevin was a student, not technically enrolled in Urqhardt's class, but a student nonetheless, an English major, nineteen years old. Urqhardt was forty-one. His sexuality exempted him from certain aspects of political correctness (no one in the administration wanted to confront a tenured gay professor about anything, least of all his love life) but even so it was impolite, he thought, to so flagrantly disregard the rules. More than that, he'd worried that Kevin would be bored. It was the idea of Kevin out with his friends on New Year's Eve, instead of at Urqhardt's side, that convinced him in the end. This generation, these boys, they were wild in ways that made Urqhardt both envious and afraid.

"All these married people," Kevin said.

Urqhardt considered that perhaps now was the time to take Kevin home, before the party lost its novelty and charm. They could rent a movie on the way, buy a bottle of grocery store champagne, greet the coming year curled up tipsy on the couch. But the thought of the apartment unnerved him all over again. It was as if the robbery had made him aware of something dreadful that he'd been ignoring all his life, the dark potential of empty spaces, the true and fearsome nature of ordinary objects. Instead, he said, "What's so interesting about married people?"

"The very notion," Kevin said.

Urqhardt scanned the party, this woman, that man, the lot of them chattering away, teeth flashing, voices rising and falling, like someone was fiddling with a knob. The room blurred a moment, returned to focus. At his side, Kevin smelled of bourbon and body spray.

"So you're not ready to call it a night?"

"I have a better idea," Kevin said.

Evan

Evan decided to take a break from the computer. His heart was still pounding from Miss Anita's interruption and he couldn't quite catch his breath. He stretched out on his bed. His mind was racing. He thought about Veronica. He thought about Lulu Fountain, how he'd shanked a soccer ball into pep squad practice this one time but instead of kicking it back, Lulu had picked it up and walked it over and placed it gently, like something fragile, into his hands. He thought about the woman on the toothpaste commercial. He thought about the tormented damsels in Lucifer's Gate. He thought about Veronica again. hotbush.com offered a link called the VIP Room where for the *LOW, LOW PRICE OF $9.99 PER MINUTE* he could chat in person with the girl of his choice while perusing her *PRIVATE PORTFOLIO—HOT! HOT! HOT! BUSH AVAILABLE ONLY TO PREFERRED CUSTOMERS*. He'd been afraid to try it. He had no idea what he would say to Veronica given the chance or how much more private her portfolio could be than the pictures he'd already seen. He made an effort to put her out of mind. He thought of these bare-midriffed high school girls he'd followed at the mall last week. He thought about his retarded cousin, Sally. He thought of the redhead on the show about lawyers. He thought about the ladies in his mother's book club. He thought about the woman in his comic books who could manipulate the weather. Then, against his will, there was Miss Anita behind his eyes, her housedress and her step-ins, her black fat forearms, her round black face, her black ankles, thick as knees. He snapped his eyes open and lurched off of the bed. Who did she think she was? This wasn't her house. He wasn't her child. He was too old for a babysitter anyhow. As if to spite her, he bolted across the room and turned his fingers loose on the computer keyboard, launching himself back into cyberspace, back to hotbush.com and straight into the VIP Room with Veronica.

His computer whirred quietly to itself. Briefly, Evan considered his father's American Express bill, wondered how long before it would arrive. Then the screen flashed blank and was refilled pixel by pixel with Veronica in the shower, her right foot raised and propped on the soap dish, her left hand at her crotch, and the thought of his father's credit card dissolved. Veronica looked vaguely astonished, though not displeased, to find Evan in her bathroom. These words appeared below the image: *I'm in the shower, sexy. I'll be right out. Why don't you tell me what I should wear.*

Evan nearly logged off. He forced himself to con-centrate, shut his eyes, tried to imagine what a man in his position ought to want from a woman like Veronica. The only man he could think of at the moment was his father. He pictured the photo of his parents hang-ing in the hall outside his room.

A wedding dress.

Kinky. What's your name?

Evan.

How's this, Evan?

The shower scene vanished. In its place appeared Veronica in a long white veil and white pumps and that was all. She was smearing cake icing on her breasts.

I'm so hot. I want your big hot cock.

OK.

Where do you want to put your big hot cock?

Blink, blink, blink went Evan's cursor.

Where would you like me to put it?

I want it in my mouth. I want to suck your big hot cock.

The image shifted, this time to Veronica on all fours, her backside looming. She was looking bug-eyed at the camera over her shoulder. There was a peeled banana in her mouth.

It's so big and hot and hard.

Between his legs, however, Evan could only manage half a wood. He jerked himself with his free hand, to no avail. He worried that he'd worn himself out for good, wondered if it meant there was something wrong with him that he couldn't keep it up for a woman like Veronica.

Tell me what you want, Evan.

Blink, blink, blink.

Do you want Veronica on top?

Veronica appeared on-screen astride a saddle. She was pinching her nipples. The saddle was on a marble floor in front of a blazing fireplace.

I'm riding you. Make me cum.

Evan stroked himself wildly, felt the pressure of frustration building in his chest. He was red-faced, panting. He was limp now as a sock. He went at it a minute longer, then bounced himself off of hotbush.com and back into his room. He could see his face reflected in the monitor. His hair was mussed like he'd been asleep, damp with sweat at his temples and his brow. The familiar, fake butter smell of microwave popcorn was seeping up the stairs and it made him hungry but he didn't want to go down there yet. Instead, he booted up Lucifer's Gate for real this time and disemboweled the devil's minions for a while.

Lulu

Lulu kept one hand on Ike's shoulder in case she needed
leverage. She could see the glow-in-the-dark face of her
watch. 9:02. Her mother would have found the letter
by now, would be in a froth of terror and anger and guilt.
Lulu almost felt sorry for her. For a long time after her
parents divorced Lulu had hated them both, especially
because there had been no sign of what was coming—
no shouting matches, no visible descent into medicated
depression or eating disorders or alcoholism. Which was
how a bad marriage looked on Lifetime and A&E, though
not always, she would admit, the way it looked in the
lives of the broken-home kids at school. As far as Lulu
could tell, her parents got along just fine. She wondered
if they were together right this minute, pictured them
clinging to each other on the sofa at her mother's place,
taking consolation for her loss in each other's company.
In a movie, she thought, her running away would re-
unite them for good and in a few years, when she and
Ike were settled, they might all look back on this night
as a necessary turning point, a blessing.

Faintly, Lulu heard footsteps on the gritty, sawdusty
stairs.

"Ike," she said.

He grunted, put his lips on hers, tried to kiss her quiet, but Lulu turned her face away. "What?" he said. He looked like he'd been hypnotized.

"Someone's coming."

Ike blinked, cleared his throat.

He said, "Who's there?" to the dark.

Myrtle Walsh leaned against the doorjamb. She was a sophomore at Bishop O'Dell, which put her three years ahead of Lulu, a year behind Ike. She crossed her arms and her ankles. She had a beer in her right hand.

"Ike Tiptoe," she said, "your presence is requested on the lawn."

That was something Lulu had noticed about Myrtle Walsh: The more she drank, the more formal her speech became. By the end of most nights at Illumination Meadows, she was enunciating like she'd learned to talk by reading wedding invitations.

"What's up?" Ike asked.

Myrtle rolled her eyes.

"The Neals and young Ollie have cornered a possum. They desire the pleasure of your company while they fuck with it."

"You're kidding me," Ike said. He stood and hurried over to where a window would have been, pushed back the sheet of plastic, laughed out loud. "Holy shit. I'll be right back. You guys hang out."

And he was gone, his feet clomping down the stairs, his voice leaping up from the lawn. "You dumb shits. That thing's probly rabid."

Myrtle took Ike's place on the bench seat, offered Lulu a sip of beer, which she accepted.

"So. Are you and Mr. Tiptoe having a lovely time up here?"

Lulu said, "Yes." Which was sort of true. She added, "So far," though she wasn't sure what she meant and hoped Myrtle didn't ask. She walked over to the window, gazed down on Ike and his friends. They were huddled together watching this big old possum amble through the weeds. When Ollie rushed it, the possum flopped over like it had fainted and the boys howled with laughter. Then they crouched behind Ike's Jeep until the possum thought the coast was clear, let it waddle a few yards farther from the house before one of the Neals came charging this time and the possum swooned again.

Myrtle said, "I always thought it was fake."

"What's that?" Lulu said.

She watched her words take shape in the cold, then disappear.

"Playing possum. That's what it's doing, the poor thing. I thought it was just some weird, old-time expression."

So had Lulu, but she didn't let on.

Boyd

"Ike Tiptoe. Ike Tiptoe. Ike Tiptoe."

Boyd Fountain listened to his ex-wife repeat the name like an incantation, like the solution to some great mystery was contained in those three syllables. They were in his car now, headed west on Old Shell Road. Boyd was fiddling with his cell phone. He needed to get ahold of his blind date, explain himself, apologize, but he couldn't make the call with Stella in the car. Haley Marchand had set it up out of the blue. Esmerelda Daza. Beautiful, Haley said. As beautiful as her name.

"Ike Tiptoe, Ike Tiptoe," Stella said.

Every night for the final ten years of their marriage, they would wait until Lulu was asleep, then creep down to the basement to hash out the day's disagreements where their daughter couldn't hear. There was always something. One night, when Lulu was away at summer camp, they were arguing beside the Ping-Pong table and the foldout couch, the air mildewy and stale, and it occurred to Boyd that nobody else was home.

"What're we doing down here?" he asked.

Stella tossed her head.

"We're talking about respect, Boyd, how you can't seem to remember you're not the only person who lives in this house."

"I mean in the basement."

Stella looked at him for a minute. Then it dawned on her and she smiled.

"It's over, isn't it," she said. "It's been over for a long time."

And just like that they stumbled onto the anti-dote for their unhappiness. Yes, it was hard on Lulu; that was the worst thing. Maybe if they hadn't done such a bang-up job hiding things from her when they were still together, she'd understand that they were better off apart.

Boyd had dated some at first but he took no plea-sure in it, in part because he felt, despite the reams of legal documents, permanently attached. He had agreed to let Haley set him up tonight only because of the woman's name. Esmerelda Daza. Esmerelda. Daza. It sounded like a kind of warm and glowing gem.

"Ike Tiptoe," Stella said.

The heat was running in the car but it looked cold outside. Steam billowing from restaurant vents. The too bright, too clear quality of the light. He wondered why winter bothered with Alabama. There was nothing redeemable about the season, not even snow or ice to make it charming way down here.

Then, suddenly, like something had just occurred to her or like she'd been thinking of something besides Ike Tiptoe all along, Stella said, "What were your plans? Where were you going when I called?"

"Nowhere important."

He could feel her staring at him. Neither of them had been invited to the Marchands' New Year's Eve party since the divorce and he knew her feelings would be hurt. He also knew—and so did she—that he couldn't keep a secret. Not from her. She kept on staring.

In a quiet voice, he said, "The Marchands'."

"Do you have a date?" she said.

He looked at the cell phone in his hand. He couldn't look at Stella.

"Not really. More a blind date sort of thing."

"Sounds like fun," she said.

Then she screamed and Boyd was so startled he dropped the phone and hit the brakes and they came skidding to a stop. He thought at first that she was screaming because of him but there was a man in a gold tracksuit in the middle of the road. "What the hell?" Boyd said. It was like he'd fallen from the sky. The man was just standing there, unfazed. He was holding a poster-board sign that said, *Repent!* in black letters. Boyd honked but still he didn't move. Boyd honked again. No response. So he backed up and drove around, went by the man on Stella's side. As they passed, Boyd gave him the finger and Stella drew the sign of the cross in the condensation on the window.

Katie

When they weren't at parties, which was most of the time, the Butters lived in a nice house in a nice neighborhood, right around the corner from their church. Hugh made plenty of money. Both Evan and Nicole did well enough in school. Katie had her volunteer work, her friends. Once a month they booked Miss Anita to keep the kids so they could have what Katie referred to as a date: dinner and a movie or a traveling production of a Broadway show. Unless Hugh was too worn out from work, they had sex on Friday nights, usually missionary, usually in bed, but once in a while they tried something more risqué, the shower maybe or Hugh's car in the garage. Until September, they'd owned a neutered cocker spaniel, but he'd been run over by a van. Katie buried him herself behind the potting shed before the kids got home from school. If she'd had her way they would have replaced the dog for Christmas but Nicole wasn't interested and Evan had his heart set on a computer.

Now, she was perched on the Marchands' couch between Lauren Killibrew and Astrid Watts. There was another woman, Esmerelda something, sitting in an armchair to her left. Katie had seen her before, talking to Urqhardt. Nearly an hour had passed since Hugh had left her in the kitchen.

"I need to find someone for kissing," Esmerelda said. She spoke without contractions, adding a lilt of the exotic to her voice. "My date, he is not coming. There is nothing more sad than a woman alone at midnight on New Year's Eve."

"What about him?" Astrid said. She pointed at a man holding a martini glass over his head, staring up into it through the bottom, as if he suspected a foreign object in his drink.

Esmerelda made a face.

In the corner by the window stood a Christmas tree, frosted white and decorated with the sort of enormous colored lights popular in the '70s. Katie wondered if it was meant to be retro or nostalgic. Tomorrow, she thought, she'd box her own ornaments and Hugh would return them to the attic and drag their tree out to the curb. Then, in a day or two, she'd inform the children of her plans and nothing would ever be the same.

"Well," Lauren said, her voice self-consciously good-humored. "You can kiss my husband if you want. If you don't find anyone. I'm sure he's tired of kissing me."

Astrid slapped Lauren's thigh, a playful rebuke.

"Which one is yours?" Esmerelda said.

Lauren aimed a finger. Mark was at the buffet table holding a meatball on a toothpick.

"My life is over," Esmerelda said.

Katie was thinking of their house in the old neighborhood, the way it creaked and moaned at night, the way she sometimes had the feeling that she was being watched, the way it was cold in places for no good reason. She'd speculated to Hugh that maybe something bad had happened there, something tragic, but Hugh, of course, dismissed her. What surprised Katie was that the feeling had traveled with them when they moved. When all the lights were out and the children were in bed and Hugh was snoring at her side, she'd lie in the dark for hours washed in nameless trepidation. This is what was on her mind when she excused herself and hurried off into the crowd before Lauren or Astrid, presuming she was headed for the restroom, could offer to accompany her. She was not, in fact, headed for the restroom. She told herself that she was looking for Urqhardt, feeling guilty about before, that she wanted to apologize for her rudeness. If she happened to locate her husband, so much the better.

Evan

Evan gathered himself on the way downstairs, prepared to look innocent and unashamed, but nobody paid him any mind. Miss Anita was sprawled on the couch with her heels in Nicole's lap. Nicole was massaging her arches, watching TV. Miss Anita's feet were fat as hams, the color of chocolate on top, caramel on bottom, her toenails hard-looking, yellow, shot through with cracks. Nicole didn't seem to mind. She pressed her thumbs into Miss Anita's flesh and Miss Anita moaned. The popcorn was in a metal colander on the coffee table, but Evan had lost his appetite.

"You got it now, baby girl," Miss Anita said.

Her eyes were squeezed shut and though she did not open them at his approach, Miss Anita turned her head slightly when Evan dropped into his father's leather chair.

"How's Lucifer?" she asked.

Evan said, "Dead."

Miss Anita popped her right eye open.

"Praise Jesus."

Evan looked at the TV. Times Square. The mill-ing, roaring masses. There was a rock band playing on a raised platform. The crowd moved like wind-licked trees. Evan felt a blush rising in his cheeks. You didn't actually get to do battle with Lucifer until the seventh circle of hell and he'd only made it to the third, where he'd been beheaded by a demon called Asmodeus. There had been a maiden in a tattered dress chained to the wall in the chamber where he died.

Nicole said, "Miss Anita is letting me stay up to watch the ball drop." She was blond, her hair chopped into a pageboy. Her hands kept moving over Miss Anita's feet. "She said I could if I gave her a massage."

"That was sposed to be our secret." Miss Anita didn't sound particularly concerned.

Evan said, "Mom won't like you up til midnight."

"You either," Miss Anita said. "We all in this together. Or we all in bed at ten o'clock."

Nicole jerked her knees and slapped the bottom of Miss Anita's foot. "But you promised. You said if I rubbed your feet I could stay up. That's what you said, Miss Anita."

"And you said you wouldn't tell nobody. Now look."

Nicole gazed at Evan with pleading eyes, her fist closed tight around Miss Anita's toes as if she'd forgotten what was in her lap. "Evan. Please."

Miss Anita did a sleepy, slit-eyed smile. "How bout it, big brother?"

Evan glared at her a moment, turned his attention back to the TV. Beside the bowl of popcorn, there were four tiny, empty liquor bottles, the kind his father drank on airplanes. He knew his parents wouldn't like that either. He was thinking of a time several years ago when he'd said something smart to Miss Anita (he couldn't remember what it was) and Miss Anita spanked him and he'd gone running to tell his mother and his mother had gotten mad at him instead. She made him write a hundred times, "I will always be polite to Miss Anita." His handwriting was clumsier and slower and loopier back then and it had taken him two hours and ten sheets of paper to get it done. Tonight, he felt like his skeleton was too big for his skin. On TV, the camera panned in on the vocalist. Her lips and eyes were done in black. Then the camera backed away and she was taking these long, spidery steps, her elbows jacked above her head, hair visible in her armpits. He wanted to head up to his room but he was afraid his erection would let him down again. He'd seen movies where cancer victims refused to go to the doctor because they didn't want to know about their disease. That was how he felt.

"I'll think about it," Evan said.

Miss Anita groaned and rocked to her feet. She told Nicole, "Don't you go nowhere, baby girl. I got

a whole nother foot needs some attention." She tot-
tered off in the direction of the bathroom. Her purse,
a huge ungainly thing crocheted with roses, was on the
floor at her end of the couch. When she was safely out
of earshot, Evan slipped across the room and unlatched
the clasp.

Nicole said, "You better not."

Evan gave her a look. There were half a dozen
airplane bottles in the purse, maybe more, still un-
opened. He picked one up and read the label. Peppermint Schnapps.

"I'm telling," Nicole said.

"Not if you want to stay up," he said.

The toilet flushed and Evan dropped the bottle
back where he had found it. It made a plinking sound.
He took another look and he would have sworn he
saw a pistol, small and black, wedged in the bottom
corner, part hidden by Kleenex packages and paper-
back books and mittens and hard candy and a key ring
that must have held a hundred keys. The sight of it
made his scalp itch. He was just reaching for it when
he heard the slap of Miss Anita's step-ins on the hardwood and he fixed the clasp and hustled back to his
chair.

"All right, baby girl," Miss Anita said, kicking her
shoes off, wiggling her toes. "You ready with those

magic fingers?" It took a minute to get herself rearranged on the couch. There was a lot of scooting and sighing and pillow smacking before she was satisfied.

Evan didn't know what to do about the pistol or the schnapps so he watched the parade of musicians on the countdown show while Nicole and Miss Anita jabbered about nothing in particular. He considered his evidence. He couldn't figure how to let his parents in on what he knew without seeming like a snoop, without getting himself in trouble, too. He wasn't even sure of what he'd seen. Miss Anita cleaned house for his mother two days a week and in the afternoons his mother drove her to the bench up on Spring Hill Avenue where Miss Anita met the bus that would take her to her neighborhood. Evan didn't know where she lived. He pictured her sitting there at the bus stop while his mother's car receded. Then he heard his name and his ear pricked up.

"With Lulu Fountain," Nicole said.

"Well, well." Miss Anita's eyelids looked like the tongues of his father's old brown shoes.

"He circled her in his yearbook. I saw it."

"I didn't make that circle," Evan lied. His skull felt huge and molten. "The yearbook was already like that when I got it."

"You love her," Nicole said.

Evan said, "I do not."

Miss Anita said, "Sometimes love don't feel like love." She crossed her ankles. "There were times when I didn't much want to love McGreggor."

Evan said "Who?" in an irritated voice. He wondered why some people had to go around saying what they thought about everything all the time. It took all his willpower not to blurt out what he knew.

"My babies' father." Miss Anita paused, pinched her lower lip. "He gone."

Evan was struck by that word—*gone*—by its mystery, its finality, and by the way she said it, like it was familiar on her tongue, but he didn't want her to think he was curious about her life. *Gone,* he thought. It was a hard word to get his head around.

"I don't love Harold Flower," Nicole said.

"You don't?" Miss Anita said.

"There's no such person," Evan said. "You made Harold Flower up."

Nicole poked her tongue at Evan. "How could I not be in love with him if I made him up?"

Evan gaped at his sister. That was such a stupid thing to say he could hardly imagine a reply.

Ike

What never failed to surprise Ike Tiptoe was how thoroughly the world tapered down upon itself when he was kissing Lulu, as if nothing existed beyond the kiss, not winter or music or Illumination Meadows, not even Lulu herself, in a weird way, except her lips and tongue and neck and earlobes and the sugary smell of her skin all mixed up with the citrusy smell of her hair.

He was absolutely divorced from his conscious self, a perfect conduit of yearning. He wondered sometimes how much this had to do with Lulu or if the feeling was born of the act itself, kissing a girl, any girl (he was handsome in a pale and slender way, almost pretty, and had kissed his fair share), for hours on end, without the hope of satisfaction. Lulu had made her boundaries clear to Ike and though he was always testing, his forays into her shirt or toward her panties were little more at this point than a way to occupy his hands. He was convinced of her resolve. This might have been a deal breaker under other circumstances but there was something about Lulu, in the purity of her restraint, that separated her from other girls, that made the act of kissing her an end in itself. He had approached her that first time, at the homecoming game (Lulu in her white mittens, her pleated pep squad skirt, her tights), in part because he hoped a younger girl might be grateful for his attention and in part because he'd already kissed most of the girls worth kissing in his own grade.

More than a month had passed since then and here he was, loitering in the depression under the curve of her jaw, listening to, without registering, the tiny noises she made, hardly more than vibrations in the back of her throat, a sound like the instrument of some lost Pacific Island tribe, when suddenly Lulu pulled away and asked him, "Do you love me?"

"What?" he said. "Yeah."

This wasn't the first time he'd said the words to Lulu. Lulu wasn't the first girl. And he meant them in his way, inasmuch as he understood that he felt something for Lulu (the others, too, though the sensation was different in each case) which might have been love. He didn't know. He thought about his parents watching TV every night until they fell asleep, his mother on the sofa, his father in the armchair, the living room quiet but for laugh tracks and/or dramatic music, depending on the hour, not a single word passing between them.

Lulu dropped her eyes now and chewed her bottom lip. Her lips were puffy from all that kissing. This was maybe an hour after the boys had finished with the possum and everybody had gathered downstairs for a beer, after they'd rehashed the whole adventure a few times (which had culminated with the second Neal bolting out from behind the Jeep for his turn, except the possum stood its ground instead of playing dead, bared rows of pointy teeth and hissed and chased him back into the house), after Ike had smoked a little weed. He'd taken Lulu's question in stride (he knew from experience that girls needed plenty of reassurance) but the next thing she said caught him off guard. She raised her eyes, pushed her hair behind her ear.

"I ran away from home."

Ike blinked and wiped his mouth with the back of his hand. This was something that needed to be addressed—that much was clear—but he couldn't quit staring at the cross hanging in the hollow of her throat.

"I don't get it," he said.

"There's nothing to get. I wrote this letter for my mother. I mean, I told her everything, how much I love you and all and how much she's a bitch. Then I cruised before she came home from work and hid behind the Dumpster til you picked me up."

Ike said, "For real?"

"For real."

"Dude," he said.

Lulu said, "I know."

They were quiet for a moment, meaningfully so. There, Ike thought. That was that. She thought something had passed between them. It didn't matter what it was. He was already leaning in, shutting his eyes, anxious to get back to the business of her lips and neck and earlobes and the faint, hot flutter of pulse beneath her skin.

Roland Tiptoe met them at the door in a V-neck sweater and pajama pants. He wasn't wearing a shirt so his chest hair was unbridled. His eyes were rheumy and obscene. Boyd put on a smile, explained the situation, wondered if Tiptoe knew where they might find his son. Stella was standing behind and to his left, looking past both men into the house, shag carpet right up to the door, dead ficus in the foyer, TV muttering somewhere out of sight. No sign of Lulu.

"That's a nice car," Tiptoe said.

He pointed at Boyd's Mercedes, craned his neck to get a better look. The house was a redbrick rancher on a block of identical ranchers in a neighborhood featuring more of the same.

"Thanks," Boyd said, "but listen—"

"Is that the new one?"

Boyd said, "Yes, but—"

"I went to the dealership the day those came out but they wouldn't let me do a test drive. My credit didn't clear."

"That's too bad," Boyd said, "if you could just . . ."

But Stella wasn't really listening anymore. She was wondering instead how this man Tiptoe had produced a son who so filled Lulu up with love that she was willing to throw her life away. He was one of the least attractive men she'd ever seen. He was taller than Boyd by an inch or two, and a little hunched, as if his head was too heavy for his spine. When he spoke, his Adam's apple jumped around in his neck. Boyd was no movie star, that was true. He'd gone soft around the middle and under his jaw. His nose had gotten pulpy over the years. But he still had his hair and his posture and his stodgy way of dressing suited him, made him seem distinguished, and under no circumstances would he be asking irrelevant questions about cars or anything else if he was in Tiptoe's shoes. It was hard to stay mad at him for not telling her about the Marchands' party, about his date. He was here with her now.

". . . so you understand we don't want to make trouble for Ike," Boyd was saying. "I'm sure he's a good kid. And you better believe I remember how it was to be his age. We're just worried about Lulu. That's the thing here, Roland. We just want to find our daughter."

Boyd cupped his hands together and rocked back on his heels, his summation posture. Stella had seen him many times in court. They were waiting for Tiptoe to reply when a woman shouted, "Ro-land," from somewhere in the house. Tiptoe flinched.

"What?" he shouted back.

"You better come watch this."

"We've got people here. I'm right now talking to these people on the porch."

The woman said, "I've never seen anything so sad."

Tiptoe made a face and stepped outside. He was just pulling the door shut behind him when a white Pekinese darted through the crack and down the steps and on into the yard. They watched as the dog sprinted three tight loops around the Mercedes, stopped, took a moment to catch its breath, then sprang onto the hood and curled into a ball as if to sleep.

Katie

There was no sign of either man on the sunporch or the deck. Katie made her way upstairs, her feet falling between half-finished cocktails and crumpled napkins and discarded coats. Halfway up, she passed a single red high-heeled pump. A hallway branched off from the landing. Katie could see four doors, all closed. The first opened into a closet. She was about to try the second when she heard a toilet flush. The door swung open from the inside and Donna Mason stepped out.

"Katie Butter!" Donna squealed at the sight of her and planted a kiss on her left cheek. "I know we're supposed to do our business downstairs but did you see that line? Well, of course you did. Here you are."

Her eyes were puffy and bloodshot and Katie wondered if she'd been crying.

"Is everything all right?"

Donna waved her hand before her face as if swiping at an insect. In the old neighborhood, the Masons had lived three doors down. Both Lee and Donna were known to be good cooks, collectors of folk art, infertile.

"Allergies," she said. "There's a cat somewhere in this house. Listen, we haven't gotten to catch up. I'll wait right here for you to finish. Then we'll hide out and swap stories. How's that sound?"

Katie said, "It sounds great, but Lee is looking for you." The lie came so easily it felt almost a thrill. "I saw him just now. You go on."

Donna smiled again, kissed her cheek again. She held Katie's face in both her hands. "I'll find you," Katie said. She moved into the bathroom, listened for Donna's footsteps on the stairs. When she was certain that Donna was gone, she crept down the hall, pressed her ear against the next door, heard mumbling, motion. Her heart bumped and swelled. She knocked once, then pushed the door open. The room was dark and Katie saw a great, vague heaving on the bed. There passed a moment (electric, strangely hopeful) when she believed that what she saw was Hugh and Haley Marchand. Then the shape on the bed untangled itself and Katie realized that she was hearing only male voices. She backed into the hall and shut the door.

"I am so, so sorry." No answer. She waited a few seconds before continuing. She'd come this far. "Professor Urqhardt? I know this is awkward but I've been looking for you. May I come in? Is everybody decent?" She heard whispering. "I won't take too much time."

"What do you want?" Urqhardt said.

"Well, first off, I wanted to tell you I'm sorry for being rude. I guess my mind was . . . I was pre-occupied, I guess. And I've been feeling rotten ever since."

"Who is this? What are you talking about?"

"It's Katie Butter." She drummed her fingers on the door. "Remember? I'm coming in, OK?"

Katie closed her eyes, stepped inside, hesitated. When no one shouted at her, she opened her eyes again. A lamp was burning on the nightstand now. Urqhardt was running a comb through his hair. Kevin was tucking in his shirt.

"What is it?" Urqhardt said.

"It's just that you were telling me about the way it felt when you came home from the movie, like you knew someone had been there. I was hoping maybe you could describe the feeling in more detail."

Kevin said, "You're talking about the robbery?" He didn't seem the least embarrassed by the situation. Katie nodded. Without thinking, she began to make the bed. She fluffed the pillows, smoothed the sheets. To Urqhardt, she said, "You told me you felt a presence?" She drew the blanket into place.

"That's right." He looked flustered, suspicious, unsure of her intentions. "It's hard to describe. It was like, I don't know—"

"Like the apartment was haunted," Kevin said.

"That's not it, not quite." Urqhardt squinted at her, palmed his brow with his right hand. "This is what you wanted to talk to me about?"

"I'm leaving my husband," Katie said.

Kevin said, "Oh my."

Miss Anita

Both Evan and Nicole dozed off well before midnight. Miss Anita sat there looking at them. There was nothing more beautiful than a sleeping child. Even the boy, she thought, hardly a boy anymore and filled up with desire. What a thing, desire. She remembered how she used to slap McGreggor's face sometimes when they made love, how terrifying it was to lose herself in the way he made her feel, how feeling that way made her angry for reasons she couldn't understand. McGreggor, with his broad back. McGreggor, who threw a clot and died. McGreggor, whose mother wanted him to have a white man's name and wasn't nobody whiter than the Irish.

She remembered, too, this one time she was waiting at the bus stop, when a man in a trench coat walked up and exposed himself. He was wearing a jockstrap with a clown face painted on it, his pubic hair dyed blaze orange. That was worse somehow than if he'd been wearing nothing at all. Her stomach lurched and her feet went cold. McGreggor had been in the ground ten years by then but she'd felt his absence in that moment like a craving.

Because she could think of nothing else to do, she'd shut her eyes and prayed.

"Tell him that you love him," Jesus said.

"Is this really Jesus?"

He did not dignify her question.

"Tell him that you know exactly how he feels."

So she did as He directed. Right away, the man's eyes brimmed up with tears. He looked at her a second, then took off running down the street, his trench coat billowing out behind him like a cape. Miss Anita was, as usual, grateful to her Lord and Savior but even so, she went over to Kmart the next morning and started the paperwork on a gun.

Now, the boy stirred in his father's chair and drew his knees up and tucked his fists under his chin. He mumbled something. According to the clock on the mantel, this year was nearly spent. And her husband was dead. And her babies were grown. And look at that boy right there, so beautiful and dumb. Miss Anita pushed unsteadily to her feet. Six empty miniatures were lined up on the coffee table like long, translucent bullets and she was feeling their effect. They'd left her nostalgic, a little melancholy, but also expansive and aglow.

She touched the boy's shoulder, leaned in close.

"I love you," she whispered. "I know exactly how you feel."

Evan

Evan dreamed, predictably, of Veronica and Lucifer's Gate. Except that the circles of hell were not dungeons or chambers of fire but the rooms of this house and the rooms of his school. Except that Veronica wasn't always Veronica. In certain rooms, the school cafeteria, for instance, or Ms. Hempel's class, she was Lulu Fountain, her new braces, the dusting of freckles on her nose, the perpetually embarrassed look upon her face. But somehow she was also and always Veronica at the same time. She said the kind of things that Veronica had said. She said *big hot cock* no matter whose face she was wearing. She said *make me cum.* Her dialogue was distracting, made it difficult for Evan to focus his attention on the demons he was supposed to kill. One might expect that these demons took the form of Miss Anita in the dream but this was not the case. They were run-of-the-mill video game demons, horns on their heads and talons on their hands and gaping, fang-thick maws. Sometimes dreams only seem predictable. In Evan's dream, Miss Anita was nowhere to be found.

Lulu

Lulu's parents decided to get divorced when she was away for two weeks at summer camp. She was nine years old. They'd driven her up into what passed for mountains in north Alabama, dropped her off at Camp Rising Fawn like everything was normal, waved a smiling farewell from the windows of the car. By the time they picked her up, they'd called it quits. As her mother described the new life Lulu would lead when they got home, her father nodding and grinning sad/friendly at the rearview mirror, she couldn't shake the image of the two of them sipping a cocktail on the deck, her father turning to her mother and saying something like, "Well, I guess it's about time we packed it in." Back in reality, her mother craned around in the passenger seat and said to Lulu, "We love each other, we just don't *love* each other anymore. Does that make sense?" And, while it didn't make even a little bit of sense to Lulu, she couldn't help feeling oddly thrilled at first. This was before anger and resentment settled in. She felt like a character in a movie of the week who was about to embark on what she would later remember as the most formative and meaningful period of her life.

Earlier tonight, as she'd let her pen go raging across a piece of lavender stationery, as she trotted down the steps and tucked herself out of sight behind the Dumpster, she had felt much the same way. She had emerged from that first important stage, battered and changed but better for it, wiser, more mature, and was setting out on a new course, a more permanent one, maybe the one she would maintain forever, through marriage (successful) and children (more than one; Lulu had always wanted a little sister, someone who would annoy her half to tears but whom she loved and who would learn all about life's hard road from Lulu's example) right on through to a heartbreaking but glamorous death, something that would waste her away, leave her thin and pale with Ike weeping at her bedside.

At the moment, though, with Ike licking the hollow of her throat, she was trying to ignore an impending sense of dread. She focused her attention on "the incident of the possum," which is how her English teacher, Ms. Hempel, would have described it, tried to sort out what the possum might have "meant" in a larger sense. Lulu liked Ms. Hempel. She was young for a teacher, halfway pretty. She was weird about "Miz," not "Miss," and she cultivated a melancholy air. Just last week, they'd done a section on themes and symbols in English at Immaculate Conception. Lulu was a cracker-jack English student. The idea of both life and literature as puzzles to be solved fit her notions of the world. From somewhere in the back of her mind came the word *hibernation*. Didn't possums hibernate? Shouldn't this particular possum have been snugged into a little den somewhere, dozing through the winter? If so, maybe the fact of its being present and awake at all was significant. And there was that phrase, "Playing Possum." All by itself it sounded like the title of a mediocre romantic comedy featuring a Ms. Hempel type, only prettier, Hollywood-pretty, a teacher or a librarian or something, a transplanted Southern girl living now in some big city, who was only pretending to sleep through life. At night, she would take off her glasses and slip into a little black dress and high heels and break hearts all over town. Only what she wanted, though maybe she didn't know it quite, was for someone to come along and love the librarian side of her instead of the knockout party girl. And maybe that someone had been right under her nose from the beginning.

The trouble was Lulu couldn't make any of these interpretations fit her situation. The "incident of the possum" was just something mildly humorous that happened on this night and the only thing it seemed to reveal was that Ike and his friends were ordinary, idiot teenage boys. Which returned her to that impending sense of dread. After all, Ike had hardly risen to the occasion when she told him she'd run away, hadn't even come close to recognizing the symbolism of her actions. Namely that she had chosen him over her whole previous life. He'd simply stared at her a moment, then socked his tongue into her mouth. Maybe that meant something, too, something good, but Lulu had her doubts.

She cupped her hands over his shoulders, heaved him back. It was like trying to lift a sack of mulch.

"What?" he said.

"Do possums hibernate?"

Ike said, "How should I know?"

Lulu sucked her braces. Another word occurred to her just then: *marsupial*. She thought maybe she had her facts mixed up.

"Can I stay with you tonight?" she asked.

"Hunh?" A question. As if the idea that she would need a place to sleep hadn't occurred him until now. Then, "Hunh." The answer, in shorthand. "My dad might be cool with it, but Mom? I'm still on thin ice for stealing her tequila."

"Will you stay with me?"

Her heart was bang-bang-banging in her chest all of a sudden. Her hands tingled with fear. They had arrived at the pivotal moment, she thought, the moment when everything would be revealed, and here Ike was gaping at her like a retard.

"Where?"

"I don't know," she said. "Here."

"It's freezing," he said.

Lulu said, "It's romantic. We'll keep each other warm."

Ike looked at her a second longer, then chucked her on the arm, his features morphing into a smile, as if she was pulling his leg and he was just now catching on.

"I gotta whiz," he said.

Though of course she didn't know it yet, Lulu would remember this moment, that smile, for years to come and it would occur to her each time that perhaps Ike was only pretending not to understand what she wanted, how she felt, and her heart would break all over again in new and different ways.

Stella

Tiptoe said he knew a place where Ike went with his friends and he'd take them there on the condition that Boyd would let him drive the Mercedes. Two things struck Stella about the situation: first, that Boyd agreed, that he didn't figure a way to connive the information from this man without capitulating, and second, that Roland Tiptoe had a better idea of where to find his child on New Year's Eve than Boyd and Stella. She was in the backseat with her ex-husband. Tiptoe was behind the wheel, his Pekinese curled up on the passenger seat.

"This leather's gorgeous," he said.

Stella looked at Boyd, pinched his thigh.

Boyd said, "Where we headed, Roland?"

Tiptoe said, "You'll see; not far," and Boyd settled back in his seat like that was just the answer he'd been hoping for. But they'd already been on the road for twenty minutes and Stella no longer recognized any landmarks. On her right: a strip mall, half the store-fronts boarded up. On her left: a wall of pines. Though she couldn't see them, she heard the periodic roar and hiss of jet engines overhead. It occurred to her that her husband was afraid of Roland Tiptoe; that's why he'd avoided a dispute. Boyd was Mister Confrontation among people like himself, whose method of negotiation he understood, whose likely reaction could be gauged. In court, he was known to be dangerous and sly. But take him out of his element and his spine dissolved. She was thinking in particular of a summer evening when Lulu was still a baby. Boyd was home early from work and they were pushing her in a stroller around the neighborhood when a black man in a 280Z came roaring down the street. As he passed, Boyd shouted at the driver to slow down; all the neighborhood husbands yelled at reckless drivers. Much to Boyd's surprise, however, this driver hit the brakes and backed up in a hurry and rolled his window down. "What did you say?" His voice was rich with anger. Boyd repeated himself. Meekly. The driver went on a tear. "You don't tell me what to do, motherfucker. Don't nobody tell me what to do" and so on. When Boyd opened his mouth to speak, the driver said, "One word and I will get out of this car and beat you down before your wife and child." He stared until Boyd lowered his eyes. "That's what I thought," the driver said. Then he roared off faster than before and neither Boyd nor Stella ever mentioned the scene again.

Nobody liked to see the underside of someone they loved, she thought. Love was too hard an illusion to maintain.

Stella tipped forward in her seat.

"I like your dog," she said.

She was just extending a hand to scratch his head when Tiptoe said, "Grouch might be little-bitty but that's one of the meanest dogs you'll ever meet."

As if he recognized a cue, the dog lifted his head and growled at Stella. She withdrew her fingers. The dog couldn't have weighed more than fifteen pounds.

Tiptoe said, "I've seen him back a pit bull down."

"No kidding," Stella said. Those gin and tonics had left her hangovery and raw.

Tiptoe grinned at Boyd in the rearview mirror. "This car." He shook his head, amazed. "It's like riding on air."

He made a left, past a subdivision sign that read ILLUMINATION MEADOWS. The trees had been cleared as far as Stella could see and the houses were all dark. As Tiptoe wound farther into the neighborhood, she noticed that most of them were unfinished, plastic sheeting over gaps in the exteriors, frames exposed. They looked like the houses children draw, all straight lines and empty space.

"The developers went belly-up last year," Tiptoe said. "Maybe you read about it in the paper. Construction's on hold indefinitely. I don't know how my son and his friends found it but they like to come out here, make trouble."

It occurred to Stella that he was going to kill them for Boyd's Mercedes. Tiptoe would make her watch, she thought, while he slit Boyd's throat and did who knew what to her, then he would bury both of them right here in the ground. She'd never see her little girl again. When the developers had gotten their money problems sorted out, a construction crew would come along, pour a new foundation over her grave and she was sure that no one, not Lulu, not anybody, would ever know how or why she died.

Then she saw the shimmer of candlelight in one of the houses and she recognized the shapes of cars parked in the grass, humps of deeper darkness silhouetted by the night. Tiptoe cut the headlights, eased the Mercedes off the road, sagged back into his seat.

"That was a dream come true," he said.

They were quiet while Tiptoe savored the moment. It didn't take long for the heat to bleed out of the car. Satisfied, Tiptoe reached over, snatched Grouch out of the passenger seat, stepped into the night. They watched him striding toward the house, the dog tucked under his arm. He brushed aside a sheet of plastic and disappeared.

"Are we supposed to follow him?" Stella said.

Boyd cracked his knuckles, a hollow gesture.

"I don't know," he said.

Stella frowned, hesitated, thought of Lulu. She was embarrassed for them both. She shouldered the door open and followed Tiptoe. The air was thin, sharp with cold. It pushed under her clothes, seemed to push right through her. She heard a car door close, and Boyd came hustling up behind her. They were almost to the house when Tiptoe emerged with a kid in a sheepskin coat, the kind cowboys wore in cigarette advertisements.

"This is Ollie," Tiptoe said. "Ike's friend."

Grouch was wheezing in the crook of his arm.

Ollie said, "Lulu's a great girl."

"Is she here?" Stella said. "Where is she?"

She could feel her heartbeat in her skin.

"They had a fight or something," Ollie said. "Ike took her home. You just missed her."

Stella sagged against her husband. Tiptoe did a toking gesture with his fingers and tipped his head in the direction of the house. "They've got some weed in there," he said. "I'm gonna stick around a while." He wiggled his eyebrows up and down.

Ollie stared at him a second.

"I guess that's cool," he asked.

All the way back to her apartment, Stella admonished herself: How was it possible that neither she nor Boyd had considered the possibility that their daughter would come home? She had the sense that if she concentrated hard enough, if she worked backward through the years, past her antiques business and the divorce, past Lulu's birth, past the day she met Boyd, worked her way all the way back to when her life was still her own, she might be able to trace a pattern that would lead her forward again to this moment, her ex-husband huddled close against the wheel of his expensive car, the world getting more familiar by the mile.

Urqhardt

Professor Urqhardt was contemplating straight women. Were they all crazy? That's what he wanted to know. Were they all selfish and rude? Did they view gay men as rivals or as some sort of second-tier allies, always at their beck and call in a timeless conflict with straight men? First this one, Katie Butter. Then the other one, Esmerelda what's-her-name. Now the Butter woman again. Minutes before he'd been pressed up close to Kevin, his lips brushing the stubble on the back of Kevin's neck, and now this woman was perched on the edge of the bed, crying into her hands while Kevin patted her thigh and said the kinds of things one said in such a situation.

"Let it out. It's OK. That's right, sweetie."

He looked to Urqhardt for help but Urqhardt scowled and pushed his fists into his pockets. Kevin scowled back, like somehow Urqhardt was in the wrong here, like he was the one being insensitive. Urqhardt jangled his keys in an irritated manner.

"I'm sorry," Katie said. "It's just, it seemed so real when I told you."

Kevin said, "There, there."

Urqhardt had met Kevin at a coffee shop on Old Shell Road. He didn't realize he was a student at the time, though if he'd given it a moment's thought, he certainly would have suspected. The coffee shop was walking distance from campus. And Kevin was exactly the right age. But all Urqhardt could think about was how beautiful he looked when he pushed open the door—the hooded raincoat, the neat goatee, his left ear dangling a small gold hoop. And the way he walked, that rolling gait. He was like a strange, gay pirate, unsteady on dry land.

That was back in April and they'd had the whole summer together, undisturbed. Kevin was knocking out his language requirement. Some nights he spoke only broken, beginner Spanish. Then fall and Kevin's friends returned to campus and he started running around with them again. Urqhardt made room for Kevin's other life. He couldn't hold his youth against him. When Kevin complained about money, Urqhardt invited him to move in. When he stayed out late and the apartment was quiet and Urqhardt was sprawled in bed alone, he thought, *Let u and v be variables such that u is restricted to a proper subset of real numbers*. He thought, *Let the dependent variable y be a function of the independent variable x, expressed by y=f(x)*. He thought of Newton and Leibniz. He thought of the two Bernoullis. He thought of Euler and Lagrange and Gauss and Cauchy and Riemann.

Urqhardt understood that he wasn't a great mathematician; otherwise, he wouldn't be teaching undergraduates in Mobile, Alabama. But he consoled himself with the notion that without someone like him, without someone to understand and admire the beauty of these other men's work, the work itself would be lost.

Katie sniffled, blotted her eyes, dropped her hands into her lap.

"I'm sorry I'm such a mess." She looked at Urqhardt. "I'm sorry I walked in on you. I'm sorry for everything."

"Don't leave him," Urqhardt said.

Katie blinked and pushed the hair out of her face.

"I don't understand," she said.

"Don't leave him," Urqhardt said again, quieter now, his voice almost a plea.

Esmerelda

She was aware of all the people waiting in line outside the bathroom door, but Esmerelda refused to rush. She wondered if the men in the hall were listening to the trickle of her urine, if the sound inspired or disgusted them. Some men preferred to imagine that beautiful women had no worldly needs. Esmerelda preferred to imagine that her blind date had caught on fire. In an effort to boost her confidence, she stepped out of her panties (black, silk) and stuffed them in her clutch, then flushed and took a moment to admire her reflection in the mirror. She reapplied her lipstick. With the tip of her little finger, she smoothed her eyebrows into place. She was known to have remarkable eyebrows.

The following is a list, in alphabetical order, of the men who had asked for Esmerelda's hand over the years: Douglas Arbuckle, Jacob Bond, Yan Ding, Albert Dejournet, Preston Ford, William Little, William Locke, Rafael Manzanerez, Curtis Roper, Buckman Threadgill and Suyanarayana Vangabandu. They had loved her for a while. Perhaps some of them still did. True love, she thought, was tragic.

She drew a breath and stepped into the hall, rustled past the shuffling, shifting line. Each man went still as she passed, his discomfort momentarily forgotten. There were women waiting as well, of course, but they vanished in her presence. She had a secret now and it restored her power and she was borne forward on the strength of it, back through the party and out the front door without bidding a single farewell.

The night was clear and cold. She could feel it between her legs. Cars were lined up on both sides of the street. There was a man standing alone on the front lawn with his arms crossed. He appeared to be admiring the neighbor's holiday decorations: the glowing icicles along the roofline, the spotlit nativity, the luminescent reindeer capering on the grass with old Saint Nick. It looked like they were selling something. She took a place beside the man, felt him double-take. His glasses reflected the lights. His left hand was curled over his right bicep in such a way that she could see his wedding band. She let him be the first to speak.

"Tacky," he said.

"You are waiting for someone?"

"That's right," he said. "Our host and hostess."

"Not your wife?"

She tapped his ring with a fingernail. He pushed his hands into his pockets. Across the street, the lead reindeer's nose was blinking on and off.

Esmerelda said, "Take me home."

"You need a ride? I've got my cell phone. I'd be happy to call a cab."

She met his eyes. She did the smile.

"Oh," he said. "Wow. Really?"

"It is almost midnight," she said.

The man stared at her for a long moment.

"Listen," he said. "I mean, I'm flattered and all and you're so incredibly—" He paused. "You're kidding, right? This is a joke. You're making an idiot of me."

"You are doing that all by yourself."

"I'm sorry." He withdrew his left hand, waggled his ring finger. He blushed, like marriage was a shame. "I love my wife."

"What's your name?" she said.

"Hugh. Butter. Hugh Butter."

"Happy New Year, Hugh Butter."

And with that, Esmerelda strode off into the night. She wobbled ever so slightly when her heel sunk in the grass but regained her balance and ticked on toward her car with light from the neighbor's yard playing in her hair.

Evan

Evan woke in his father's leather chair with an erection pressing against his zipper. Miss Anita was shaking his shoulder.

"Wake up, big brother," she was saying. "It's almost midnight. Wake up, boy. Hey."

Evan recoiled, brought one arm up to cover his face, dropped the other into his lap. He was at once relieved and embarrassed by his erection. He wondered if Miss Anita noticed. She straightened up now, put her hands on her hips. Behind her, Evan saw two more empty miniatures on the table.

"The new year has arrived," she said.

He heard distant voices counting backward—*eight, seven, six*—located them on TV. An old man with dyed black hair was on stage now leading the chant. *Five, four, three.* A glittering golden orb descended a silver pole. Nicole was slumped against the arm of the couch, her jaw hanging open. Evan felt creepy, distant, half-lost in his dream.

"What about Nicole?"

Before the words were out of his mouth, the band cranked up and fireworks lit the TV night.

Miss Anita shook her head. "They been a lot of new years before this one," she said. "They be a whole lot more for her." She chuckled and clapped her hands and did a little shuffle with her feet. Evan thought she was drunk. He'd seen his father after a couple of martinis but he didn't act like this. "Praise Jesus," Miss Anita said. She snatched up her purse and danced around behind the couch.

"Time don't never stop," she said, high-stepping into the hall. Evan heard the front door open. He looked at Nicole. She was breathing deeply in her sleep. He pushed to his feet and followed Miss Anita, found her on the lawn, glaring at the stars as if they'd offended her somehow.

"Ain't no fireworks out here." Her voice sounded too loud among the pretty houses, the magnolias, the somnolent sedans. Her words took shape, like ghosts, and lifted on the air. Evan shivered. His skin prickled at the cold. "Can't have no new year without no fireworks," Miss Anita said. She dipped her hand into her purse, rooted around. This time she brought out the pistol, wet-looking in the moonlight.

"What are you doing?" Evan asked.

Miss Anita smiled at him over her shoulder. Her eyes were swimming in their sockets. She looked almost sad.

"We alive," she said. "Time don't never stop but we alive."

With that, she raised the pistol over her head and fired three times into the sky. Dogs erupted all over the neighborhood. After a moment, lights began to flick on in nearby windows. "You alive and baby girl alive and my children all alive," she said. She uttered the word—*alive*—in a noisy kind of whisper, like she was afraid of jinxing it by saying it too loud. She fired twice more over her head. "Miss Anita *alive*," she said. It occurred to Evan that the countdown on TV was in New York and he didn't know if he'd been watching a tape delay or if there was still another hour until midnight in Alabama and he felt outside of time all of a sudden or like time was something insincere, his legs filled up with air, his heart loose and throbbing in his chest. He thought of Veronica and of Lulu Fountain. The canopy of trees along the road looked menacing and lovely, bare branches like women's fingers, like demon arms. Miss Anita fired again, and Evan flinched. He doubted that his parents would let her off the hook for this, and before too long his father's credit card bill would be arriving in the mail. There would be consequences for both of them. But after that . . . but right now . . . He didn't know if the world looked so peculiar because he was still seeing it through the scrim of his dream. His lips were parted and he could feel the look of wonder on his face.

Katie

She found Hugh outside with the Marchands. Paul and Haley were on the front stoop, arm in arm, watching him waltz an enormous plastic Santa Claus across the yard. Apparently, he'd swiped it from the neighbors. Paul and Haley were laughing and cheering him on. Paul draped his free arm over Katie's shoulder.

"What a jackass," Haley said but she was clearly delighted. She cupped her hands around her mouth and hooted. "Do you tango? Lambada? Do you know the forbidden dance of love?"

Hugh dipped the Santa Claus, pressed his lips into its beard.

"I'm a fool for you," he said, beaming. He swung his gaze toward the porch, saw Katie standing there. His smile, she thought, flickered. Then he bugged his eyes in a comical way and clapped a hand over his mouth. "Katie, please. I didn't mean for you to see this."

"Busted," Haley said.

Hugh dropped to his knees and spread his arms and bumbled toward her over the grass. The grass glittered with moonlight and frost. Katie said, "You'll stain your pants," but Hugh kept coming. In his eyes, she saw passable imitations of penitence and love, and she felt a rush of affection for her husband. He'd pledged himself to her forever. He'd been that brave once, that hopeful. "Please," he was saying. "Please, Katie. Give me another chance, Katie. I love you, Katie." He repeated her name like a password, like a charm. "Don't leave me, Katie. Think of everything we've been through, Katie. Think of everything we've shared."

Paul and Haley were in stitches. Hugh flung himself down, kissed her ankles. She thought about Professor Urqhardt. She thought about Evan and Nicole, sleeping now, she hoped, secure in their bones that the coming year wouldn't be any different from the last. And it wouldn't be. She knew that. She wasn't the sort of woman who left her husband. Besides, who could say that this thing haunting her marriage wasn't part and parcel of love, no matter how it frightened her? It was cold enough that winter was seeping through her stockings but Hugh's breath, begging forgiveness, was warm.

Twenty minutes before her parents arrived, Lulu strolled over to the window and gazed out at Illumination Meadows, heels together, toes and knees angled out, First Position in ballet. She could see Ike over by his Jeep, the moon at his back so he was pissing on his shadow. She twisted the chain of her cross around her thumb. There were two options open to her as she saw it. She could take the devastated and passionate route, rant and rave at Ike or maybe pitch herself out the window right this instant and plummet to her untimely death. Thereby signifying her disillusionment. For mystery's sake, her last words could maybe be "Oh, the possum." Or she could go the way of quiet dignity. No anger. No public tears. She could simply descend the stairs, bid a fond farewell to Myrtle and Mary Lee and the two Neals, then head on out to the Jeep, where, in a quivering but controlled voice, she would tell Ike to drive her home. When he protested, she would persist. She might say, "I love you but I don't *love* you anymore," and he would somehow understand. She would suffer silently for who knew how long (months? years?) but eventually time would blur the pain and she would emerge the stronger for her heartache.

Without Ike pressed against her, the cold was creeping into her hair, under her fingernails. Her teeth were chattering and she couldn't make them stop. She could almost hear, then, the timid sound of her key in the front door of her mother's apartment, could almost see relief flooding her parents' faces, washing over them with such enormous force that everything would be forgiven. It seemed almost simpler just to let herself tip forward and out the window. Except she was only maybe thirty feet from the ground, and how embarrassing would it be if she survived?

Beyond the window, out there, skeleton houses and swaths of clay and moonlit kudzu and broken-up hunks of concrete as far as she could see. One day, someone would come along and finish this house, this neighborhood. Trees would be planted. Dogs would fill the night with their barking. This very room might well sleep a child. She pictured a little girl, couldn't help it, saw, like a time-elapsed movie shot, mint green paint going on over the walls, a border of stenciled roses, pale curtains breezing at the windows, matching dust ruffle, plenty of pillows on the bed.

Nothing was real, she thought. Everything was a symbol for something else.

Lulu was asleep on the sofa when they arrived, covered neck to knee with an old afghan. Stella lurched in her direction, stopped herself halfway across the room. The coffee table was littered with crumpled tissues. There was an empty bowl balanced on her stomach; the spoon had fallen on the floor. Tears, Stella thought. Ice cream. My daughter is in pain. In sleep, her face was smooth, her skin unmarked by time. Stella could make out the little girl in her features. Her feet, at the other end of the blanket, were battered-looking, her toe-knuckles swollen from ballet. She looked like a magician's trick, two separate bodies severed and fused. Boyd cupped his hands over Stella's shoulders from behind.

"Leave her be," he said. "We'll sort it out tomorrow."

All of a sudden he was in charge again. Stella was too relieved just then to hold anything against him. They went into the kitchen and she put a pot of decaf on. While they waited, Boyd pulled a chair out for her at the kitchen table. He sat on the other side.

"It's strange to think about," Stella said. "Right now, right this minute, there's a burglar out there."

What she meant was that the world was a perilous and random place, that life could go sour without warning. A burglar could show up at your door or a man in a sweatsuit could step out in front of your car or you could find yourself in an abandoned housing development with a crazy person. Or love could die. Or not. Or your daughter could know sadness. "He's probably wearing Professor Urqhardt's pocket watch," she said.

Boyd said, "Or Mrs. What's-her-name's tiara."

"I wonder what he's doing for New Year's Eve," Stella said. "Even criminals must get lonely."

"Particularly at the holidays," Boyd said.

Stella propped her elbow on the table, her chin upon her fist.

"Do you need to call your date? Or the Marchands? Do you need to tell somebody where you are?"

Boyd shook his head.

"They'll get along without me."

And for what seemed like a long time, with their daughter in the next room sleeping off a broken heart, they sat at the table without speaking. Stella closed her eyes, tried to sort out what she was feeling. She thought she should be grateful, sad, angry, something, but it was more complicated than that. What she could feel, what she could be sure of, was memory swimming around behind her eyes, her whole life in there, the whole history of everything she loved.

Acknowledgments

Thanks to my agent, Warren Frazier, and my editor, Elisabeth Schmitz, for endless guidance and hard work. Thanks to early readers Jim McLaughlin, Tom Franklin and Shannon Burke. Thanks to the University of Tennessee and the University of Mississippi; without the time and support provided by those institutions this book could never have been written. Thanks to John Zomchick. Thanks to Barry Hannah. Portions of this book have previously appeared, sometimes in very different forms, in *Climbing Cheaha Mountain: Emerging Alabama Writers, Christmas in the South, River City* and the *Southern Review,* and I would like to thank everyone involved with those publications, especially Joe Taylor, Don Noble, Charlotte McCord, Judy Tucker, Kathy Pories, KK Fox, CD Mitchell and Brett Lott. Thanks always, always, always to Jill, for her vision and for her patience, as a reader and a wife. And to my daughters, Mary and Helen—here's hoping they'll one day understand why Dad is occasionally so distracted and so strange.